NATURAL COMPLEXIONS

D. Harlan Wilson

ISBN 978-0-9931955-8-7

Equus Press
Birkbeck College (William Rowe), 43 Gordon Square, London,
WC1 H0PD, United Kingdom

Cover, typeset & design: lazarus.
Composed in 9pt Futura Light, composed by Paul Renner in 1927.

NATURAL COMPLEXIONS

D. Harlan Wilson

EQUUS

"One touch of Nature makes the whole world tin."
—**Marshall McLuhan**, *Culture Is Our Business*

DISCLAIMER

Most instances of gun violence have been omitted from the following document in an effort to approach something like diversity. Herein lies the fictional element of my project.

—A. Bauer, Interlaken 2017

ACKNOWLEDGMENT

Many of these docufictions were extrapolated from actual news, spam, advertisements and other detritus as well as conversations with Chris Benton, whose artful rants provided me with chronic sustenance and infotainment.

Any resemblance between the characters in this book to persons living or dead is a matter of consequence, entropy, and the natural complexions of our United Physiognomy.

TOP STORIES

ACT 1
INDOLENT SUICIDES

ACT 2
TRANSPARENT IDOLATRIES

Randolph Pierre
Maxwell La Fleur
Lillian Gish
Martin Costello
Josh Hartnett
Kris Kristofferson
Glen Campbell
Father Bauer
Poppy Trowbridge, Sr.
Vinnie Cambodia
"Gretchen"
"Grover"
Candice Veranda
Ernst Lanzer
Bertha Pappenheim
Hans Little
Dr Armand Siddiqui
Hugo Camacho
Dr Fanny Moser
Juan de Zumárraga
Sergeant Bauer
Joel Osteen
Ma'jik
Kevin Foucault
Dr Joe Levinas
Craig Barthes
Teddy Horkheimer
B.G.
Lincoln "Larry" da Vinci
Claudia "Carrie" Spiegel
Anthony "King" David
Cole Montgomery
John Travolta
Glenn Freebird
"Kawika"
"Halana"
"Wilikona"
Saul Flechsig
Hélène Kuragina
Anatole Kuragin

Natasha Bolkonsky
Andrei Bolkonsky
Lisa Bolkonsky
"Ron" (not God)
Gianna von Clamm
B. Harrison von Clamm
Dale Rabinowitz
Gordon Speck
Zarathustra
Herovit Bogg
Janine Sokolowski
Jack McGinnley
Sebastian Angle
Dominus Bauer
Angelica Bauer
Bernie the Pharaoh
Keith Moon
Colonel Kurtz
Captain Ahab
Darth Vader
Richard Nixon
Jean-Paul Sartre
Erwin the Cat
Detective Gonka
Detective Bauer
Daryl Folkenflick
Bill Steinberg
Archibald Wink
Maizy Smith
Embeth Bruns
Nelson Tyco
Brenda Diamond
Gil Stoppard
Marisa Stillwater
Dennis Diamond
Cornelius Stillwater
Dr Nathan Benway
J.J. Marvel-Ann
Leonardo DiCaprio
Zoe Gamma

ACT 1
INDOLENT SUICIDES

The Wind from Nowhere

Tracy Berringer outran the law for much longer than the aesthetes or the admen. Bereft, they adopted her stance and made grooves in her wake.

It was in fact by accident that two plainclothes officers from the Hairy Florida precinct discovered her performing fellatio on a minor celebrity who claimed to be a close relative of Tracy's in a peculiar attempt to justify the act of public fornication. For her part, Tracy claimed that the wind had blown her out of Jacobson's department store while she still had the article in her possession, and once she found herself on the sidewalk, naked and estranged, she made a quick decision to slip into the shadows, if only to avoid confrontation, rather than release the article from her clutches and return it to the store, a gesture of goodwill that would once again put her in jeopardy of being blown back outside, which may or may not result in more articles attaching themselves to her person and following her into the sun.

One question lingered in the mind of the commonwealth like an old whore: *Where did the wind originate?*

"Wind, after all, doesn't impulsively spring to life in some distant corner of a department store and then wreak havoc up and down the aisles," quipped Hawgstrüffel Media correspondent Andrew Salvadore, who happened to be shopping for cologne at the time of the incident and witnessed its unfolding.

At first, Tracy insisted on the primacy of a crossbreeze produced by a constellation of left-open doors, but wind had been blowing at a paltry 9 mph at the hour of the day in question, and even if there had been a hurricane outside, the doors were simply too far apart—and the department store too vast in its interior—to entertain any sort of meaningful draft. Soon enough, Tracy gave up and played the cards of ignorance. She continued to maintain that she had been swept off of her feet, literally, and indeed all of the footage of the incident showed her rolling across the floor with her signature tartan skirt thrown over her head; she took out two perfume girls at the knees and then disappeared through a revolving door like tumbleweed at dusk. The prosecuting attorney foregrounded the awkwardness of Tracy's exit, trying to make a case for the exit being a complete sham and an embarrassingly bad excuse for shoplifting, but it looked too real to be unreal, and the defense counsel had prepared compelling videos of people throwing themselves down small hills and rolling to the bottom in order to simulate what could only happen under the auspices of gravity or a terrific gust of wind.

"As there are clearly no hills in Jacobson's," deduced the counsel, "the latter must be true."

Nobody mentioned demonic possession, although the possibility, as always, was on everybody's mind.

In the end, Tracy received a sentence of three years on probation, 400 hours of community service, and a small fine.

Derring-Don't

During the press conference, the ex-president discussed the "resolutely adventurous" state of his disease with candor, grinning politely at reporters even when they pressured him to talk about his genitals. No question was taboo, and he answered them all. Afterwards several bodyguards escorted him outside where a fast-moving parade had been arranged in his honor. As if sensing the ex-president's attention, a float barreled out of control and ran him over, mangling his limbs and breaking his neck. He died on the scene. Footage revealed that the bodyguards neither hurled nor shoved the ex-president into the float's path while making no attempt to protect or shield him from harm's way. Approximating an exploded ventriloquist doll, the corpse remained pink and febrile until an EMT vehicle arrived and paramedics took it away. The collective sigh of disappointment was almost powerful enough to topple gravestones.

Jekyll v. Hyde

Deranged by years of drug and alcohol abuse, Sudden Infant Death frontman **Gary Indiana**, 44, can no longer tell the difference between his real and onstage persona. Hawgstrüffel Media broke the story. Indiana talks and refers to himself in what he calls the "sixth person," denouncing the first, second and third person points-of-view as "Dead Rituals" (the title track on SID's most recent album), and staring dryly at paparazzi who ask him what happened to the fourth and fifth persons. Accused only last month of glamorizing colonialism in a video that depicted the band in bleached white safari gear gunning down bushman with large caliber rifles, Indiana's "Personality Breech" (the fourth track on *In the Land of Aholy Christs*) comes at a bad time. His girlfriend, Home Shopping Network hostess **Dolly Bee**, 26, made a public statement yesterday explaining how she felt like a demonic presence had infiltrated and overtaken his body. His sister, art school dropout **Indigo Avalon**, 52, confirmed Bee's statement and added that the windows of his eyes no longer expose his soul; rather, they expose the truth of the afterlife: "Nothingness." One of his twelve aunts, homemaker **Sarah Ford**, 65, fainted when the cameras pointed in her direction but later filed an affidavit backing up the claims of Bee and Avalon. His mother, **Gabby Fortinbras**, wife of real estate mogul **Arny Fortinbras**, 72, passed away over a decade ago at the age of 59 from complications with rheumatoid arthritis. Indiana (in his current state and in all former iterations) admitted to being haunted by her "Evil Ghost" (the only track on the album of the same name, 62 minutes long, sung in an insidious a cappella whisper) for tormenting her as a child. At the same time, he has told at least fifteen talk show hosts that he was a "Product of Neglect" (the track that marked his only solo venture) and acted accordingly for somebody with a big heart who craved attention and didn't get it. Bee and Avalon think he needs to go to a rehabilitation facility; at the very least, he should solicit a priest for an exorcism. "Effort leads to effect," noted Indiana's therapist and rumored lover, 46-year-old **Dr Thérèse Papyrus** (of the font dynasty). In the meantime, a court-mandated restraining order has been issued against the so-called sixth person in hopes of ousting him from the scene after photographs of bruises, lacerations, and other evidence of self-mutilation surfaced on SID's website.

Communiqué

Fat swung from her neckline in misshapen pouches as "Gloria" waddled across the stage to a microphone and explained how the gland exacerbated a condition that had always been irreparable. She concluded on this note: "I only eat 1,100 calories per day." Everybody clapped and she waddled offstage as "Desirae" shuffled onstage and accused the gland of sentience and misanthropy. During her *communiqué*, somebody toppled out of a chair in the back of the church and emitted a series of bored moans. Several attendees ambled to the victim's aid. In spite of the moans, which grew louder and louder, a pulse could not be found on the wrist or neck, and when "Janice" spread all of her fingers onto the heart, she smiled and died.

In the House of Quo

This was the description on his dating profile: "My name is Quo and I am in my house." The only other detail was a response to the section entitled **What I Do Very Well**: "Pirouettes." She wondered if the lack of information annoyed her more than the available information. And yet she had not received an image of his penis. That was a good sign. If nothing else, he had not broken the Golden Rule.

NEVER SEND A WOMAN AN UNREQUESTED IMAGE OF YOUR PENIS.

But did he understand the Second Rule?

WHEN A WOMAN REQUESTS AN IMAGE OF YOUR PENIS, DO NOT SEND HER THE IMAGE OF YOUR PENIS. INSTEAD, RESPOND WITH SOME VARIETY OF WITTY BANTER THAT BOTH DEFLECTS AND REIFIES THE REQUEST BUT DOES NOT NECESSARILY SATISFY THE REQUEST.

And what about the Third Rule?

GOD IS A DOG THAT LICKS THE STINK FROM MY FEET WHEN I WALK INTO A ROOM AND KNOCK YOUR SOCKS OFF.

The Fourth is more important than the Third.

I WILL BURY YOU LIKE A TURD IN A DIRTHOLE.

Eyeballing the specter of insecurity, she decided to take a chance and write Quo a message.

The best medicine is not to exist in the first place ...

She wondered if she should send the message with or without the ellipsis. And if she didn't use the ellipsis, would a period be the thing? An ellipsis would signal an omission that either indicated something to follow (e.g., something meaningful) or alluded to *outright uncertainty*. A mere period, on the other hand, would bear the stamp of confidence, closure, *downright certainty* ... What kind of man did she want? A man who wanted the ellipsis and what it may or may not signify vis-à-vis the maxim in question? Or a man who wanted a period? She assumed that most men wanted periods. Periods were concrete. Periods were strong and overconfident. Periods demonstrated a wild, rugged simplicity. Periods explained themselves, stood for themselves, asserting their identity by presence alone. The bullseye on every target was a period, big and black and round and indisputable. No ambiguity about periods. And yet Quo wasn't like the others. He was in his house, and he did pirouettes very well ...

As she contemplated sending the message to Quo, she received a message from Quo.

Hello! You look great. What are you up to tonight?

... the tyranny of little men ... but is there any other form of tyranny? The only tyrant is the Little Man. David—not Goliath—was the prototype ...

P.S. on Suicide Note (Third Draft)

... kill the ego and liquidate the anxiety, the death-phobia. Become comfortable with being uncomfortable. Be kind but deflect bullshit at every turn. Buy a stranger a tank of gas. Push forward. Manifest a clean, clear body and exhume being-in-itself from the grave of culture and hyperreality ... This must be the Last Exposé, Pops. My strongpoint has always been my capacity to do nothing, even on those fair-weather occasions when I love you madly and pretend not to be an actor. Now I have skirted oblivion. Rest assured, I am real because I am dead.

L. Ron Hubbard's White House Tapes

For the photograph, the author did not merely rest his chin on the shelf of his hand and peer sideways with casual purpose and resolve. On the contrary, he extended his thumb and index finger into an L-shape and slid his hand up his face, cupping the chin with the thumb and pressing the blade of the index finger into his cheekbone. Consequently he redefined the wizened wrinkles of his good eye. It was not until the flashbulb went off a sixth time that the cursing struck a meaningful pitch. Parents shielding their children's ears only made the author more incensed and hateful, and yet he maintained the pose, notwithstanding the movement of his flytrap lips and the vibration of his vocal cords, even when his face turned purple and a rhizome of veins inflated on his forehead and neck. This could only go on for so long. Eventually he lost consciousness, tipped sideways and slammed into the floor with the force of a girder from the sky. Nobody knew what to do; even the resident pediatrician stood there dumbly as a final hiss of air escaped the author's lungs like an evaporated prayer. Inspired, the photographer took several more pictures, moving around the author in a wide arc, then closing in with brisk and flamboyant two-steps, as if the author were a fallen disco ball that would not give up its spinning, glittering ghost. As he skipped back to a tripod to reload the camera when he ran out of film, the author awoke with an eerie roar, and he resumed cursing precisely where he left off, nostrils flaring to the size of quarters. Bystanders on the periphery slipped behind curtains and darted out exit doors. Getting to his feet, the author returned his hand to his face, locking the L-shape back into place, but the effort threw him off balance and he fell down again. Writhing and screaming, he beat his ham-fists against his chest and pounded the heels of his penny loafers into the floor. His agent stepped forward to deliver an invective on behalf of the publisher of his latest book, but he hardly broke silence before the author belittled and shamed him for being no better than a lawyer or a politician or a road floozy, especially the latter, who possessed far more cultural capital than him, not to mention brains, balls and sand. Moments later the author stood over the unconscious body of the photographer. The room was clear, and so was he.

How to Smile like the Joker

Brad Schmidt begins to dry himself in the shower stall before turning off the water. This has happened before.

He had dreamt about the large woman again. She sat in a rocking chair in the dining room of the cottage with her misshapen family pushed against the walls. Whenever he leaned over to kiss her on the cheek, her head disappeared into the broad dunes of her shoulders. It was embarrassing. He could feel the family growing increasingly bitter and anxious about his failure to land the kiss. One can't kiss what one can't touch. Palsied, Brad Schmidt excused himself and found the bathroom. He turned on the shower, removed his clothes, unfolded a towel and began to dry himself before entering the stall ...

It worked in the dream. It doesn't work in the real world.

Brad Schmidt turns off the water and wrings out the sopping towel. Dripping, he exits the stall and gazes into the mirror. He smiles. It's not a good smile. But that doesn't matter. According to the advertisement for the seminar, one doesn't need to possess inherent smiling talent. If one has a "good" smile, one has a leg up, but even with a "bad" smile— even if one has never smiled before, says the ad—one can, with sufficient practice and a little luck, smile like the Joker.

He has air-dried by the time he arrives at the seminar, towel in hand, and pays the coolie half of the enrollment fee. Proctors circle the amphitheater like plucked buzzards as Dom Romero delivers a lecture on poise and shows everybody how to organize the lips in such a way that the corners retreat into the ramus of the mandible and catalyze the teeth. Brad Schmidt claps and hoots with the audience, even though it is obvious that Dom Romero has inborn smiling endowment and experience while claiming to be a virtual neophyte.

Near the conclusion of the demonstration, somebody raises a hand

and asks how to laugh like the Joker. Proctors swarm and forcibly remove the insurgent as Brad Schmidt, irrigated by the pathways of happiness, nervously begins to dry himself.

Selfie Blues

Pertaining to the selfie she had captured in the front yard of the burning house: it was the neighbor's house, and she liked the neighbor in spite of his ungainly physique, loud barbeques and occasional stalkings, but when something is on fire, or when something is generally in peril, default logic requires a digital memory of the chaos that foregrounds the self.

She posted the selfie and skipped inside.

The fallout was immediate.

Followers and friends hashtagged her **#flamingbitch** and **#fieryslut** and **#scorchedcunt**, as if putting out the fire with a bucket of water had been a viable option for her. There was nothing to be done; the house would have burned to ashes anyway. What was the harm in an innocent selfie?

Within minutes, her identity had not only usurped the fire, it had become the fire.

An angry horde congregated outside of her house before the arrival of firefighters, police and paramedics. They used the neighbor's house to light torches and threatened to smoke her out if she didn't take action against herself. She took pictures of the mob from an upstairs window and posted them. No reaction; her virtual audience had evidently put faith in Karma's rancor. She expressed her frustration with a sequence of melodramatic emoticons as a fusillade of Molotov cocktails crashed through the windows and exploded onto the walls, floors and furniture. She tried to escape, but everybody shot at her with their rifles whenever she opened a door or climbed onto the roof. Dejected, she clutched her phone, dove onto a burning couch, went up in flames and, in so doing, went down in history, putting herself out ...

The Book of Widows

The pages feature Polaroid stills of widows that date back more than 50 years. They appear happy, posing in finely manicured yards defined by picket fences and woodbox gardens. Only with concentrated scrutiny can one detect anything resembling sorrow or grief in their physiognomic stances. In the basement of the church, Beatrice Flaux skims through the book and recognizes an old girlfriend from college. Her name was

Elizabeth Spooner. They belonged to the same sorority and once fingered each other in a gazebo during a party, drunk on grain alcohol. Elizabeth's scent had flooded her nostrils like tear gas. Sometimes the scent rushes back to Beatrice. All efforts to identify a palpable mnemonic trigger fail her and she remembers what her mother used to tell her on Sunday mornings: "Only your unconscious knows the truth." She doesn't smell anything right now as she examines the image of her sorority sister standing alone beside a mailbox with her arm shoved down the waist of a wool-knit skirt; knees bent, eyes pinched, head thrown over her shoulders—Elizabeth is grinning like a worm. This supposed gesture of authentic bliss troubles Beatrice, who recalls how dark and dystopian Elizabeth's worldview used to be. One never recovers from what one is. Clearly the gesture indicates an effort to evade or altogether escape her true identity. There is also the issue of her dead spouse. Beatrice can't empathize with people who pluck the fruits of joy from the tree of death. Even a good death. Even the death of a bad man.

And My Benighted Ambiguity

Doctor Bauer prepares to read and expel the emotions trapped inside of his patient's internal organs. He drapes the patient across an adjustment table and grips the divining rod of her arm at the wrist. He spreads his powerful legs, breathes evenly, and invites LOVE into the foyer of his consciousness.

"BRIAN GONKA," he utters. "That's the first thing that comes to me. Is this person trying to hurt you? I'm getting a bad feeling. It's interesting."

"BRIAN GONKA?" says the patient.

"Yes."

"I know a Brian Schumacher and a Roger Gonka but no BRIAN GONKA. They're all trying to hurt me."

"They are?"

"Yes. They hold me in contempt for plagiarizing their dance moves and ultimately their identities."

"All of them?"

"Yes."

"That's interesting. How?"

"I don't ask questions. I only follow orders. Did I tell you that I was stalked and nearly murdered by a psychotic who I dated in high school? I used to perform sexual favors on him between classes. He told all of his friends and I developed a reputation. 'The Dream Queen,' they called me. We broke up after graduation and he pursued me for a decade, kidnapping and molesting me at least twice a year. He killed himself during a high-speed pursuit with the cops. It had nothing to do with me, but it gave me serious flashbacks."

Doctor Bauer releases the patient's wrist and takes a step backwards. Sometimes he has to do this so that new information can well up. After "BRIAN GONKA," he hadn't received anything.

"What kind of flashbacks?" he asks. "You can put your arm down. Something's coming. We need to wait for it."

The patient bends her elbow and rests her forearm across her breasts. "I don't know. General stuff. Stuff having to do with my evil powers and my damaged mythology. And my benighted ambiguity. They make me have to go to the bathroom, these afflictions. But I drink too much coffee and soda and I always have to go to the bathroom. I'm like an old man with a bad prostate."

"Interesting."

"Do you feel anything yet? Is that what you do? Feel my feelings? Or do you see them or something? Or hear them?"

"It's difficult to explain."

The patient's nipples harden and she rearranges herself on the table. "Ok."

"Precisely," chirps Doctor Bauer. "That's precisely the thing: ok. I could answer every question that anybody puts to me that way. Ok—it's a philosophy."

"Is anything there yet?"

"No. It's interesting talking to you, though. I don't talk to all of my patients like this."

"Like what?"

"You know. About demons and angles. About the holy war that's going on. About the many lives we live and leave. About your aura—how all of the emotions imprisoned in your aura are related to God, and how your Beingness carries those emotions from one iteration of yourself to the next. All that. My formal training is in chiropractics, but I'm more of a life coach and a holistic therapist. Anybody can crack your back. Not everybody can exorcize feelings from your heart, lungs, kidneys, liver, intestines and aura."

"I know."

"Ok. I'm getting something." He takes the patient by the wrist again and reads her body. "Interesting. There's anger in your heart. It's directed at BRIAN GONKA." He touches her chest and traces a line to the ceiling. "Now it's gone ..."

Historiography

Religion was the gene. Gastromancy, according to the Greeks. They believed the gongs of indigestion might belong to the articulations of the dead, the ghostly, the spectral or the cosmic. Long ago, a dyspeptic became a seer, interpreting the gastrointestinal bedlam like a fortuneteller. The congregation hung on every word that his spastic colon brought to bear. It wasn't until religion gave way to entertainment that spokespeople introduced a prosthetic extension into the equation. This happened in the eighteenth century. At first, bored carnies formed talking heads with their fists. Soon men in suits had usurped the stage and were performing several nights a week to sold-out bandwidths. Inevitably the human became redundant. Then utterly superfluous. Recall every episode of *The Twilight Zone* in which a man in a suit loses his mind. Consciousness is a virus and the price of inoculation is death. Subsequent generations believe that they can do better, but in the end, everybody dovetails into a weak-kneed abyss. From the box we came, smelling of bong resin and synthetic rubber, and to the box we shall return.

Poppy Trowbridge

The alias used by **Tracy Berringer**, 32, to reserve hotel rooms and obtain prescription medication was made public when police discovered that her lover, **Furio Stagg**, 40, committed suicide by ingesting a toxic combination of Percocet, Ambien and Propanolol, all of which had been prescribed to "**Poppy Trowbridge**." Initially authorities treated the suicide as a homicide and fingered Berringer for the crime, but a solid alibi, a death note, and a slew of hateful emails from Stagg's father, **Gil Stagg**, 71, put her in the clear. According to Hawgstrüffel Media, Stagg had been working as a stunt man on the set of **Martin Bach**'s upcoming political thriller *Midnight Motorcade* when he failed to emerge from his trailer one morning. Among other things, his father accused Stagg of binge drinking, maintaining a poor diet, wasting his life, and never taking the proper steps to conquer dyslexia so that he could become a schoolteacher. Stagg had unsuccessfully attempted to kill himself three years earlier when his mother, **Barbara Faragher**, 68, died of brain cancer. The day Stagg succeeded in killing himself was the third anniversary of Faragher's death. In a surprisingly literary suicide note, he discussed a number of issues, employing figurative language and at times accomplishing a musical syntactic rhythm. He mentioned Berringer frequently, referring to her as Trowbridge (viz., "Pops") and asserting that he loved her "madly." Berringer admitted to being "devastated."

She insists on paying for the funeral, which is scheduled for next week in Belfast, Staggs' place of birth, and at her behest, her brother, UFC fighter **Terry Deed**, 28, will serve as lead pallbearer. She has also lent Staggs' family—including seven full siblings, three half siblings and four sets of grandparents—"crucial moral support" since the tragedy went public. Nobody in the family blames her. Nor do they blame his father, who, in the wake of his son's death, has been placed on suicide watch, not only due to recent threats leveled against himself, but because of a history of erratic behavior and schizophrenic episodes. Since the tragedy, Berringer has kept a low profile, yet numerous photographs have been taken of her between workouts and dining engagements. The grief on her face and in her general posture could move mountains. She is said to be "inconsolable."

Oneiricana

The publisher scrapped the original title of BRIAN GONKA's trilogy of one-acts for being too cryptic and technically not a real word. "People should be able to understand book titles," was the operative logic of editor-in-chief Omar Sabat, "and neologisms are bad for business." They changed the title from *Oneiricana* to *Three Plays*, a simple but classical rendering used by publishers of some of the greatest playwrights in history (e.g., Eugene O'Neill, Anton Chekhov, August Wilson, Harold Pinter, Marquis de Sade, Euripides, Sophocles, etc.). Incensed, BRIAN GONKA went on a rampage that began in a mall and ended in the grave. His death boosted sales of *Three Plays*, but not enough for the publisher to retrieve funds allocated to the book's production and distribution, let alone generate a profit, despite considerable expenses for advertising that capitalized on the way in which BRIAN GONKA committed suicide and the ensuing spectacle of loathing and grief that swept across the nation. E. A. Juffali & Company almost went under. When rumors surfaced that the ghost of BRIAN GONKA had been haunting their offices in New York, Chicago, San Diego and Port Clinton, however, Sabat made a statement on national television that generated as much buzz and revenue as it did panic and violence. Indeed, there are global villagers who believe that the fallout threatens to alter the emotional texture of the mediascape ...

Law Enforcement Jargon

Doctor Bauer was taking a selfie when the policeman angled his motorcycle into view and gesticulated for him to pull over. Leaning a shoulder against the driver's side window, Doctor Bauer resituated himself, smiled a hangnail smile, gauged the mise-en-scène one last time, and captured an image with the policeman visible in the background, casting him in the role of a photobomber. The policeman's eyes burned in the petroleum darkness beneath the mirrored beak of his visor; in the selfie, he looked like a Francis Bacon painting that Doctor Bauer had been excited to stumble across in some forgotten corner of a curiosity shop.

"Missing person!" bellowed the policeman. "Breach of the peace! Grievous bodily harm!"

"Hi!" Doctor Bauer rolled down the window. "Hello!"

The front wheel of the motorcycle wobbled and the policeman nearly sped into a ditch. He righted the vehicle and edged closer to Doctor Bauer's Datsun.

"Drunk in public! Possession with intent to supply! Victim support scheme!"

"Victim support scheme!" replied Doctor Bauer. "That's interesting! What does it mean!"

The front wheel wobbled again. This time the policeman lost control.

Doctor Bauer pulled to the roadside, climbed into the passenger's seat and rolled out of the car. The policeman thrashed in a ditch like an overturned tortoise. Barreling towards him, Doctor Bauer got a cramp in his thigh and lost balance. He accomplished a flaccid pirouette in an effort to keep his footing, then fell down. Presuming the worst, the policeman unholstered his weapon and fired into the ether. He emptied two clips. Doctor Bauer shouted that he only wanted to examine him and check his vitals. The policeman reprimanded him, told him never to get out of his car, accused him of "braking and exiting." Besieged by the cramp, Doctor Bauer reeled in the ditch as he called 911 on his cellphone and reported the policeman, accusing him of attempted murder. Trucks roared down the highway as the 911 operator vetted him, fearing a prank caller. During the interview, a bullet entered Doctor Bauer's ear and exited his eye. It grazed his brain. The policeman stood and limped over to the perpetrator and shot him twice in the chest. Doctor Bauer arched his back and sighed like a reptile as life escaped his good eye and a thousand trapped ghosts seemed to flee the prison of his skull.

The policeman collected his phone. "No further action. No fixed abode," he told the 911 operator.

A forensics sweep revealed zero evidence of foul play.

The policeman nodded and told lazy jokes to the investigators that half-heartedly interrogated him. Gravediggers arrived, dug a hole and buried the body of Doctor Bauer at the crime scene.

A search of Doctor Bauer's car revealed a troublesome, almost offensive air of cleanliness. Not a trace of garbage. Not even a shock of hair or a clump of dirt. The dashboard gleamed. The weatherproof floor mats had been bleached, scrubbed and blow-dried at least once a week. The leather seats were immaculately detailed; only on a molecular level could detritus be observed in the seams. Even the interior of the door locks had been scrubbed and polished recently with a toothbrush.

The glove compartment contained two items: an owner's manual for the vehicle and a pair of sunglasses acquired from a Dollar Store.

There was a ventriloquist doll in the back seat so lifelike that it startled the onsite pathologist, who deduced that the doll was in fact a doll and documented its condition.

The only other article of interest was a slip of paper recovered from a pocket in the driver's side door. It had been neatly wrapped around a weathered photograph of science fiction author and Scientologist founder L. Ron Hubbard. On it was a "CHECKLIST" with six numbered items printed in crisp, brittle handwriting:

1. Make sure there are no holes in your underwear.
2. Make sure to eat complex carbohydrates.
3. Do not forget your pocketknife.
4. Do not masturbate!
5. Do not meditate!
6. Always remember who you are.

ACT 2
TRANSPARENT IDOLATRIES

Anthem of the Heart

An online *naïf* who made his name by claiming to be "hung like a skunk" passed away from a heart condition that went undiagnosed for more than a decade. In a recent video discovered by Hawgströffel Media, 12-year-old **Randolph Pierre** refused to expose himself even as he made and remade the claim, angrily throwing darts at still shots of skunks affixed to his bedroom wall. Pierre suffered from hypertrophic cardiomyopathy. His family says nothing preemptively could have been done about the condition because he never showed any symptoms. He passed away without recourse. Doctors have inspected his siblings' hearts and unanimously concluded that they are "hyperfunctional." Unchecked by destiny, they will not meet the same end.

Worms and Fleas

The cult gestated like an imaginary fetus before going public and deciding on a name.

The members wanted to liquidate every shareholder that didn't own a pet.

Their thesis: *If one fails to own a pet, one fails to cultivate the human element.*

"Animals are the apogee of company," was the cult leader's working observation.

In time, the members grew apart and the cult disbanded.

Asked how he felt about cats and dogs in a PBS documentary several years later, the defunct leader famously responded: "How do I feel about cats and dogs? I like cats and dogs, but I do not own cats and dogs. I own worms and fleas, and I will turn everything you love into garbage."

Reykjavik

"Life is a shit sandwich from which, sooner or later, everybody must take a big fucking bite. Why has this age-old proverb suddenly escaped us?"

These words in response to the Reykjavík massacre.

Practicing "an experimental form of meaningless violence," terrorists claimed to have targeted the Icelandic capital for its "virtual anonymity" as much as its "terrible beauty" regardless of the city's notoriety as the site where the Cold War saw "the first glimmerings of its demise." Magical landscapes interpose the sprawl of late-night clubs and discotheques where artists, hipsters and fashionista dance like fallen angels. The roofs over the flea market and along the river Elliðaár explode with color and resemble hard candy from the vantage point of nearby mountains. In addition to cuisine and booze, the Blue Lagoon is important; this geothermal spa reminds us of our last trip to Mars with its steamy waters and bedazzled tourists. There is a dead volcano and sculptures of emaciated Vikings that are set on fire by vaudeville stiltwalkers twice a day. What to eat: oysters, clams, mussels and shark meat. What to think: how the sunny disposition of the residents of Reykjavik collectively belies the dark angularity of winter when the sun only shines three hours per day. For centuries, Reykjavikians have been getting drunk on caraway-flavored potato schnapps, a beverage that tastes like sourdough bread marinated in high-quality octane.

"You can't say that, Mr. President," cautioned his media advisor.

"Mr. Hoover. That's the accent."

"Pardon me. You can't say that, Mr. Hoover. Shit sandwich."

The President had trained his entire cabinet to refer to him by the name of the former incumbent whose voice he threw at any given moment. He was a talented ventriloquist and perceived his own docile body as the ultimate dummy.

During the eighth retake, a paraffin lamp on the east end of the desk died out, producing an eerie chiaroscuro that reconfigured the President's face.

Valency

Zebras are the primary source of crime. Not even an antichrist can stop them. This is accurate. More to the point is the enemy that keeps watch over the gates. The process of detoxification betrays the simplicity of perception. What we need are actors who aren't afraid to slaughter real people. I am going to marry that tiger. Kris Kristofferson is likely the trendiest automaton to ever live a human life. You should have seen the man transform into a demon onstage. Archrival Glen Campbell trembled in his red presence. Nobody bothered to draw the curtains as if to conjure his Teacher into the limelight. Teachers inform all of our lives. They speak to us about Love from beyond the Veil. Any attempt to extract details about the universe results in obligatory frustration and information that can possibly damage the emotional bandwidths of users. Stay away from Ouija boards and bourbon whiskey. In combination these provisions can be deadly. They seem harmless but they are precisely the doorways bragged about by the ombudsmen in their guidelines.

Death Sentences

Sentenced to death for butchering the attendants of a dinner party that included three top-grossing movie stars, bodybuilder, socialite and neo-Victorian **Maxwell La Fleur**'s one regret was that he wouldn't be in tip-top shape for his execution, having ordered lasagna, garlic bread and red wine for his last meal the night before the long-awaited media event. In the execution chamber, he told the families of **Lillian Gish, Martin Costello, Josh Hartnett** and other victims that he had been worried about dying and extreme anxiety often prompted him to carb load. "It's actually good to drink a glass of wine the night prior to a competition," he explained with increasing enthusiasm, "because it flushes the water out of your body and you look a lot leaner. I once had a colleague who drank an entire bottle of Jack Daniels 24 hours prior to every competition, and he was like a stone god. You should drink a little hooch just before you go onstage, too—it makes the vascularity pop and takes off the edge." He paused meaningfully and hung his head. "You can't consume any other form of carbs, though. Certainly not starchy carbs. That's a toxic combination. For a man of my proportions, it's a death sentence." Asked if he had any final words, La Fleur shifted gears and apologized for the murders, but only in theory. "The deeds of yesterday are a myth," he opined, "like yesterday itself. Only tomorrow holds the promise of reality."

The Aesthetics of Seduction

Hey man. Are you tired of murder?

I know clever pickup lines and funny stories have their place. Don't get me wrong—I've seen how effective they can be in the right situations if the right people use them.

Let's be honest.

Not every guy has the natural ability to talk his way into a woman's panties. For most guys, the best-case scenario is that they get shot down right away. Worst case? She strings you along because you "make her laugh." Maybe she even gives you her number or accepts your friendship on a social network. So you might waste your time for weeks (or even months) thinking you have a chance with this girl ... when all she's really doing is being polite.

How do we skip all those games and not kill somebody?

A friend of mine recently taught me a controversial technique to seduce a woman without using any words. You won't believe it until you see it for yourself ...

Women Measured Collectively

"I am a very cheerful and charming lady. I have a good sense of humor and I love to make people smile. I like to take care of people who I love and to make them happy. I usually treat people the way I want them to treat me. I love life and I enjoy every moment of it. I adore beautiful things, like every woman does. I am a woman who combines the qualities of a successful specialist and a woman who can become the guardian of the earth. I am an optimistic woman and I know that I will find a p—"

A metallic groan interrupts the *communiqué* and incites existential dread in countless male onlookers. Substance abuse exacerbates the dread. We must now live with it. All of the cultural wishmasters have been exposed to chemical agents.

Beyond the Veil

Father Bauer goes berserk.

It happens on a weekday in the Liverpool Cathedral as tourists thread in and out of the café and stagger up and down the geometry of stairways that define the mountainous walls.

Offset by the blunt realization that he remains "merely a household God, no better than a minor deity in a soap opera," Father Bauer storms through the narrow aisles of pews and organ pipes swinging a mad axe. He wears a Force Publique jacket that he found in the prop room beneath the Lady Chapel and his breakdown is partly an excuse to wear it.

He tackles an old man, straddles his body, and raves about "God's nerves" and "divine rays" and "fleeting-improvised men" as he makes chopping motions with the axe. He has no intention of actually using the weapon—in fact, he is in full command of his dimensions and the breakdown is pure melodrama—but he accidentally exaggerates a chop and buries the axe in the old man's skull.

Cuffed in the back seat of a patrol car, Father Bauer explains himself to the arresting officers: "There are 52 original souls. These souls birthed 1,100 additional souls. I don't know why and I don't know how or when—I don't ask questions. All of us contain traces of the 1,100. Isn't that interesting? Some of us contain the full matriculation of the original 52. We have all lived billions of lives on this planet and many others. I once lived on an asteroid in the form of an alien dust mite. We all have Teachers that speak to us. It's interesting. You can call them angels, if you like. They exist in the fold of Pure Love. Every human being has one—and only one.

Teacher, I mean. They use humans as their mouthpieces and want us to be happy. Generally they are individual entities or spirits who answer to God. The interesting thing is that I don't have one of these Teachers. *My Teacher is God.* He speaks directly to and through the apparatus of my body and mind. These words I'm speaking are not my own. *They belong to God.* And I have never encountered anybody else whose Teacher is God. I say this without Ego. You may think I have a messiah complex, but I don't. I am what I am. Like Popeye—and Jesus." The policeman in the front passenger's seat strikes the divider with a fist and tells him to shut the fuck up. Father Bauer falls silent. Then continues: "There can be no light without darkness. Demons outnumber the Originals by a landslide. Their task is to lie. Their schematisms are simple, like the wiles of little boys whose parents ignore, beat or molest them. Over time, the schematisms become more complex and potent. Eventually they transcend logic and comprehension. They are like barnacles on the hull of your cunt. Interestingly, the only way to shake them is to dissuade them. And this is done by lying to them as intricately and patiently as they lie to you."

"Shut your bloody hole!"

Deported to America for impersonating an Englishman, Father Bauer explains himself to the customs officers: "I'm almost certain that I was murdered in my former life. I believe the guilty party's name was BRIAN GONKA. Possibly Roger Gonka. Or Brian Schumacher. I used to be a chiropractor. That was my cover. Really I was a healer. A protector. A life coach. Gripping my patients' arms like tuning forks, I asked their bodies questions and removed the horseshit from their organs. I can't remember when I became a priest. Am I a priest? Sometimes I forget. Bless you. In another life—possibly this life—my house burnt down, and my wife left me, and then I spent an entire year living in a farmhouse in Larne, Ireland, speaking with the Devil. Not John Milton's Satan—that Devil had cache and intellectual fortitude and a great hairdo. The Devil I was talking to— the real Devil—was a stupid asshole. A simpleton. It's interesting: I think He has brain damage. Yes, it's a He. The Devil has a Giant Cock. His voice was like a mosquito in my ear. I believe we currently exist in a kind of vat. We're falling to the bottom of the vat where it's utterly dark. Once we get there, bad fucking shit will eventuate. But then the light will come back. We're losing the light. I can barely see you people."

The customs officers appear to be taking dutiful notes during Father Bauer's soliloquy, but video footage reveals that they are only competing to see who can illustrate the most realistic-looking genitals.

Months later, on death row, Father Bauer explains himself to his fellow inmates: "Hello! Beyond the Veil is another mode of existence. It frustrates me when other human beings don't perceive my subjective experience as objective reality. I once broke a patient's arm because of her lack of belief in *my Word* as *the world*. Likewise did I only *pretend* to purge a demon from the liver of a man in light of his ideological shortcomings vis-à-vis me. It was a bad demon, too. I should have gotten rid of it despite his attitude. The thing is, I don't judge anybody, even as they judge me. My actions derive from the ground zero of Pure Love."

Seven weeks later, Father Bauer receives a pardon from a Judge whose wife he had exorcized in another life, but after he signs all of the paperwork and exits the penitentiary, a dazzle of zebras that have escaped from a nearby zoo trample him. The zebras are hunted and shot. Father Bauer is rushed to the hospital and moves beyond the Veil en route. A paramedic notes that the last word he utters, "GONKA," seeps not out of his crushed mouth but from the cone of a swollen purple nostril.

The Dangers of Hypnosis

L. Ron Hubbard's interests were not limited to writing science fiction novels, engineering new religions, and maneuvering the arch-cape of assholery like a matador as he strutted through the playhouse of existence. He was also an accomplished oenophile, preferring California to Bordeaux, and he enjoyed hypnosis as a means of "relaxation," a subject that was apportioned two chapters in his unpublished trilogy of autohagiographies collectively entitled *The San Luis Obispo Prescriptor*. He had no interest in extracting information from the people he hypnotized. Nor did he make them bawk like chickens, defenestrate themselves, etc. It was the act of tapping into their minds and putting them under the anesthesia of his power that he thrived on. Once subjects had been hypnotized, he didn't care what they did. Usually he ordered a manservant to remove them from his presence, but not before breaking the spell and inducing a vertiginous hangover that would generally wear off after a few hours of aimless peregrination. In her biography of Hubbard, **Poppy Trowbridge, Sr.**, a short-lived member of his inner circle, claimed that his hypnotic practices were as wild, egotistical and hazardous as any of his practices, especially in that his "sensei," emeritus stuntman **Vinnie Cambodia**, repeatedly told him not to hypnotize people without more training and certainly not without a reason beyond idle jouissance. Hubbard died in 1986 from a stroke at the age of 74. In a 1980 bulletin, he promised his followers that, in one of his next lives, he would come back "not as a religious leader but as a political one."

I Am Not a Man—
I Am Dynamite

"A woman's ass makes more sense than God."

Piqued by the self-summary, "Gretchen" made the first move and sent "Grover" a message. "Gretchen + Grover," read the message.

"Grover" didn't reply for several hours. Then: "Haha. Where you at?"

"Gretchen" tried to wait for at least ten minutes before sending a response in order to convey the requisite air of nonchalance. She lasted two minutes. "I live in Indianapolis. I'm a RN."

Four days later: "RN?"

Five and a half minutes: "Registered nurse. What do you do? I like what you said about God. It's funny."

Eight seconds: "It's true."

Despite sending three more messages and a booty pic, "Gretchen" never heard from "Grover" again.

Fear, Loathing, Etc.

"Good people drink good beer." The aspiring model who plowed over nearly 100 pedestrians on a sidewalk outside of Vegas Strip's Planet Hollywood on Saturday night texted this ancient Celtic axiom to an undisclosed phone number just before losing control of her vehicle. **Candice Veranda**, 32, tried to flee the scene, but bystanders jumped on the vehicle and battered her into submission. Hawgstrüffel Media collected footage from the Front Line. Yanked from the shattered driver's side window, Veranda was beaten as her daughter watched from the back seat. Several minutes later police broke up the melee and took her into custody. "I want to become a spy," she told arresting officers in a performative Southern drawl. "Is it hard?" Toxicology revealed that Veranda was not under the influence of alcohol or drugs at the time of the incident. Fatigue, malnourishment and disillusionment were the culprits. She had parked safely on numerous hotel properties, but security kept running her off. According to the police report, Veranda claimed: "It was a stressful time of day and I was just trying to relax inside my car with my daughter." She informed cops that she didn't remember driving onto the Strip or even running over people. The last thing she remembered, she said, was a body bouncing off of her windshield, shattering it. Regarding the text that allegedly initiated the accident, Veranda had no memory of its derivation, composition, meaning or recipient. Likewise were authorities unable to identify the owner of the number, although they did determine that it was not a mere clay pigeon. Someone or something had received the information.

Conditional Autosarcophagy

Brad Schmidt frowns at the cellphone and places it beside the sink. He studies the mirror. He smiles. It isn't a bad smile. It is a fine smile. A capable smile. He raises his finger and studies the wound. Last night he accidentally hacked off a portion of his fingertip while dicing the tenderloin. It got lost in the meat and he couldn't find it. The meat cost $16 a pound and he couldn't throw it out. After some consideration, he decided to cook and eat himself. Should he be worried about it? He had eaten his own toenails and fingernails and gnawed off callouses before. This was different. The part of his finger he masticated and swallowed hadn't been dead skin or keratin. He dials the number of his self-help counselor and puts the phone on speaker as he practices smiling in the mirror.

"Hello!"

Brad Schmidt tells him what happened.

The counselor berates him and reminds him about the dangers of cannibalism. He doesn't know how to diagnose or help him. Does eating oneself constitute self-cannibalism? Auto-cannibalism? Autosarcophagy? Conditional autosarcophagy? The counselor is at a loss.

During the conversation, Brad Schmidt doesn't waiver; he continues the practice of smiling in the mirror. In fact, he feels invigorated and free, as if the act of conditional autosarcophagy has unlocked something mysterious in himself.

Ahabesque

"Be wary if BRIAN GONKA happens to read the newspaper. I still can't believe that monomaniac fell so fast and so deep into such malign paranoia and Ahabesque fury. In spite of himself, he remains a fundraising juggernaut, and I don't pretend to understand the chronicle of normative actions and reactions he commits on a daily basis. Even more distressing is the fact that BRIAN GONKA doesn't cry. Does he even feel pain? Animals don't cry when you whip them, and I have seen BRIAN GONKA beaten like an Amerikan slave. What does that make him? And what does that make me? *Ein Übermensch?* I need more Kratom. Whenever I run out, I hit the bottle harder than a sailor at port. This new Cambodian blend I bought last week cleared up my senses like a *deus ex machina* on Sunday. More later."

CSI: Dreamfield

The bones were found on a path along Vienna Lake about two miles south of Dreamfield.

Lucid County Sheriff Ernst Lanzer said: "There's a high probability that the discovery made on Sunday afternoon by Bertha Pappenheim, a local nurse who had been walking her Alsatian German Shepherd along the lake, will eventually be identified as human remains."

Pathologists have conducted a preliminary exam on the found objects in a forensics lab.

Local police say that an anthropologist from another town (possibly Narcopolis) will be summoned to conduct a more thorough review.

The current review yields clues that add up to virtual naught.

"Despite the possibility of the bones belonging to a human being, a professional can often determine the age, race and sex of the deceased entity, even if the only evidence is a skeleton," said Sheriff Lanzer.

Hawgstrüffel Media correspondents talked to a deputy coroner in Lucid County about available techniques to determine from the remains how long an entity has been dead.

Deputy coroner Hans Little explained: "Is there still animal activity in the vicinity? Are there still insects crawling on the bones? Maggots? Pupae? We will collect them for an entomologist to examine and give us a better idea of how long the bones have been there."

Experts scrutinize the presence of insects because every stage in the five stages of decomposition attracts different organisms that feed on the body and recycle the flesh.

Pappenheim found the bones resting in the mud close to the water.

The remains may have washed up from the lake itself.

Pathologists will look for cuts and imperfections in the bones—or a bullet lodged in a rib or the spine—in hopes of determining if the death was indeed a homicide.

Sybaritic

Dr Armand Siddiqui ordered his technicians to replace all of his patients' scripts with placebos. As expected, patients on stronger medications reacted poorly, but the general architecture of their reactions aroused curiosity. For instance, over the course of the subsequent week, patient A, who had been ingesting 5 mg of Ativan per day, complained that it had suddenly become too easy for her to fall asleep, whereas patient B, who required 150-200 mg of codeine every four hours, and patient C, a methadone addict, both went on semi-predictable *non compos mentis* killing sprees. More compelling, however, was the behavior of patients on lower dosages and less addictive drugs. Alcohol consumption increased. Weirdly, a "movement" of echolalia afflicted 30% of patients, most of whom had no physical or social contact with one another. This led Dr Siddiqui to believe the placebo had been spiked with a control element, but inquiries into the matter revealed no tampering or trickery. Less interesting were patients on antidepressants and antipsychotics (in low or high doses) who mainly engaged in overemotional efforts to commit suicide that privileged attention over intention. "In troubled times," remarked Dr Siddiqui, "products of neglect will always resort to Shakespearean antics."

Hugo Camacho

"You better kill me good," seethed the Mexican as the sun set behind a mountain like the cart of a dumbwaiter, "or I'll be back real soon and kill you better." He had recently sailed around the spool of an atoll in the Gulf, braving storm waters in a Shanghai catamaran only to be confronted by a crew of pirates on the south side. It was 1870. Indians had fallen into the stiletto of Texas from a trauma center in Galveston, then dribbled all the way to Nicaragua. The ghosts of strung-up outlaws and back alley exorcists chased them to eternity, waving hatchets, muskets, atlatls and molotovs over their heads. This took place in the moonlight over a span of what felt like twenty years to the Captain as he reflected on the migration. He stood on his feet. Impressed by the height and density of his garbage, the Captain ordered his crew to line up outside the latrine. One at a time, they were required to marvel at the accomplishment even as the *Diablo* closed on the *Humanidad* and the Mexican reiterated his threat. Only Life's thesis responded: "Nobody gives a shit." Two days after they killed him, a photograph appeared on the front page of *El Boquiflojo*. He was a child of Byron. Smiling. Wide-eyed. Napoleonic. Pupils fixed on the bullring of sky.

The Bones of Tomorrow

The bones were analyzed by a specialist who emptied the cavities and read the marrow.

They belonged to a human being.

A human being born over seven hundred years ago.

Lucid County Sheriff Ernst Lanzer said: "There's a high probability that the discovery made on Thursday evening by Dr Fanny Moser, the New Reverie bioscientist who drew the conclusion, will eventually be identified as BRIAN GONKA."

Pathologists have given up hope despite several post-cognito exams conducted in a forensics lab.

Local police say that an osteopath from another town (possibly Port-la-Rêver) will be summoned to double-check the findings.

The current social climate in Dreamfield remains edgy and in many subdivisions frenetic.

Several residents have claimed to see BRIAN GONKA ominously loitering on Main Street outside Beer Haven and Fuse Lounge.

It is an elderly yet somehow more durable and glorious version of BRIAN GONKA.

It may be a figment of BRIAN GONKA that has passed beyond the Veil.

Evicted, he stares across the street with broken lips and a headpiece full of straw.

"In the event that the bones do belong to BRIAN GONKA, we will outsource another professional to determine when, how, why and where he was killed, even if we have to throw darts out a window and hope to find purchase in the bullseye of truth," said Sheriff Lanzer.

We talked to somebody who may have been BRIAN GONKA about available techniques to determine whether or not the bones belonged to him.

Holy diver Juan de Zumárraga divulged: "Between the desire and the spasm, between the potency and the existence, between the essence and the descent falls the Shadow."

Experts scrutinize the presence of the Shadow because every stage in the infinite stages of death and rebirth attracts different organisms that feed off of the body and recycle the flesh.

BRIAN GONKA rests in the mud close to the water.

He may have washed up from the lake itself.

Parapsychologists will look for tears and deficiencies in the fabric of reality—the proverbial "open zipper in the sky"—in hopes of determining if BRIAN GONKA is indeed BRIAN GONKA.

ACT 3
SUPERFICIAL RESURRECTIONS

Alpha v. Omega

Resurrected as a "common man," Sergeant Bauer became a motivational speaker specializing in up-and-coming alpha males. He patterned himself after televangelist Joel Osteen, who always began his sermons with a joke and the same rhetorical admission of desire, "I like to start with something funny," which he articulated in a toothy, soporific Texan drawl. Sergeant Bauer began every session with his own truism, which he articulated in a barreling yet kindly brogue: "I am not a man—I am dynamite." While Reverend Osteen concluded his sermons not with another joke but with a New Wave prayer designed to convert nonbelievers to Christianity, Sergeant Bauer asked his listeners to join him in an abridged version of his initial assertion: "Man—dynamite." What happened between the alpha and the omega amounted to a superficiality with varying degrees of import and disquiet.

Is Ahab, Ahab?

"Dear sir. Hello! The earth has stopped turning and now there is no gravity. All of the water is floating into outer space. That's what happens. From the island of Nantucket, I watch the evacuated walls of the Atlantic Ocean rise all around me into the cataract sky. Once again we must ask myself: Is Ahab, Ahab? I finger my beard and touch my great stomach. Blubber is underrated, like me—tough, elastic, compact, close-grained and toxic. I admit that my gaze is vaguely carcinogenic, although I have never killed anybody by looking at them. Between you and me, a sudden personal interface has prompted me to gather humankind into the fold of my warm and canny embrace while there is still world enough and time. I don't care about the ubiquity of Zarathustrians—they will follow the water to the moon. And the lava will follow them. It is only when I am melting that my extremities become operative and virile. I am an electromagnetic earthfucker. Fueled by 20 grams of Maeng Da Kratom, I must take the reins and dig in my spurs yet resist the temptation to ride this galactic whore too hard too soon. I will not deny anything or any thong. In the end, only a woman's ass makes sense, as they say. I know you understand and accept this artless truth."

Seduction Program

Oi compadré!

It's been a few days since I introduced you to Ma'jik. My inbox has been flooded with success stories. I know for a fact that Ma'jik intends to close the doors on his incredible seduction program soon. I want to share his tricks with you before it's too late. You might relate to my friend Kevin Foucault's story:

This video hit me hard. I'm fiftysomething, divorced, and my wife left me to be with her masseuse, who I had paid six months in advance before I found out they were screwing around behind my back. Since we separated, I've been unhappy and stuck in a rut. Dating isn't the same as it was when I was a young man. I felt lost. There's nowhere for an older guy like me to meet women that doesn't make me feel like a pedophile or a peeping tom.

Turns out Ma'jik's program was all I needed.

I have successfully used this program to enjoy late-night fun with several ladies in my town, including my hairdresser and this girl at work. Now my friends are drooling over my new, hot girlfriend!

Dr Joe Levinas is a successful surgeon. He comments:

I am very smart and I make a lot of money. I am slightly overweight. I have been single for almost two years. I recently used Silent Seduction on a hot nurse who works on my floor. She took an interest in me right away.

I followed your steps and in less than two hours we had gone from the break room to hooking up in my living room. This shit works.

It's interesting when you hear a fancy surgeon saying "this shit works." LOL.

Craig Barthes wrote to say:

I will use this technique on every girl I meet. It is dynamite. I love watching their faces get turned on from the very first second. Even my brother used it to get a girl. He is a registered sex offender and it still works.

Teddy Horkheimer sent me these words:

I knew a chick for three straight years. She would not sleep with me because she didn't want to ruin our friendship. So the other night I invited myself to her place to watch a movie and used this trick. Before midnight, she was so turned on that she couldn't even keep me from taking her clothes off. Things got extremely naughty. Three years and this is the one maneuver that got her into bed.

Finally, here is a female perspective that Ma'jik himself shared with me yesterday:

He was a complete stranger. I met him on a train. In minutes, we went from an innocent handshake to a surge of pleasure shooting down my back and up my inner thighs. It felt so good! I thought I might go crazy right there in front of him.

These are just a few satisfied customers. There are hundreds of more success stories sitting in my inbox. You'd have to be out of your mind not to give *Silent Seduction* a try!

The only thing is, you have to act fast.

Do you want to add your name to the Ma'jik Wall of Fame?

Don't put this off any longer. It may already be too late.

Peace.

—B.G.

Ennui (Part 2)

11:36 p.m. Anonymous reportage indicates that **Lincoln da Vinci** and **Claudia Spiegel** are currently involved in yet another fracas, this time at the Wynn Hotel in Las Vegas. It's happening right now in the casino; underneath the red chandeliers, the power-couple rampages across an archipelago of blackjack and roulette tables. A memetic tsunami floods the studio, caricaturing the rhetorical and physical brutality with finesse and acuity even as it unfolds. 11:35 p.m. Carrie: "Is that your Jeep in the street?" Larry: "Yeah. I parked my brand new 80-thousand-dollar billet-silver Jeep Rubicon in the street. There were no valets so I just parked it in the street like a goddamn redneck. Stupid bitch!" Carrie [*hysterical*]: "Where were you! Where were you! You were with that skank! You're fucking her!" Larry [*gesticulating at a pit boss*]: "Somebody get this cunty broad away from me! Somebody kill this fat whore! Fuck you! Fuck you!" 11:38 p.m. Policeman cuff Lincoln da Vinci as he vomits a clear, viscous substance onto the bloody, knocked-out body of Claudia Spiegel, like a fly preparing to ingest an insect. The substance appears to be acidic and burns through her skin. They drag him kicking and screaming out of the casino, and by 12:30 a.m., he is booked and quietly reading *The Wall Street Journal* in a drunk tank.

Ennui (Part 1)

Larry met Carrie at a Mexican restaurant in northwestern Ohio. She was tending bar and he was reading an old issue of *Swamp Thing*. After his third frozen margarita, he could pronounce all of his syllables. They talked about how their first names rhymed. He asked her to come over to his place when she was done with work and check out his comic book collection. She arrived before dawn. They kissed and made love on a sectional couch that kept sliding apart beneath them. "I *really* like you," Carrie told Larry. She had been drinking earlier and brought her own stash of Crown Royal. She told him not to call her "baby" during sex. Only

"Carrie" would suffice. If he liked, he could call her "Claudia Spiegel," the screen name she would adopt once she moved to California and became famous.

"It was my great-grandmother's name," she disclosed. "Isn't it beautiful?"

"I'm heading West, too, baby." He couldn't stop calling her "baby." "I'm used to saying 'baby,'" he admitted.

After he came in her mouth, she beat him for several minutes, slapping him across the face, punching his nose and stomach, and giving him Indian burns on his forearms. Periodically she enjoyed springing into his arms and leaning backwards into a kind of mad ballroom dip. He entertained the aggression until she bit him on the chin and drew blood. Collapsing onto an ottoman, she said she needed to get home to her live-in boyfriend, a "skinhead warrior" who would harangue her if she stayed out too late. Larry urged her not to drive. Carrie rebuffed him. He made her drink two espressos and a tall glass of water, fucked her in the foyer to rattle her senses, told her he loved her, and sent her on her way.

God Is Good

On Thursday, Sergeant Bauer went to Dubai and delivered a speech to the International Congress of Chinese Orthopaedic Association's most prestigious musculoskeletal experts.

"Listen to me," he intoned. "It is not a good idea to kill your ex-wife's boyfriends when they molest your children. As you beat them to within a cunt hair of their life, however, be sure that God is singing through your arms like a swooping death-bird of fate. Cancer runs rampant in my ex-wife's family and most of the women die young. And when my ex-wife finally got cancer and died like an old prune in some forgotten attic, I experienced unquantifiable euphoria to which nothing in this world or the next will compare. It's interesting. All of the heartache she gave me and my children, all of the horseshit she dragged us through so she could have her way and fuck everything with lungs, all of her bitching and complaining and sidewinding and menstruation-induced hysteria—it wasn't only worth it, I would forfeit my life savings to endure all of it again, one-hundredfold, if only I could reclaim what I felt when she died on that cot, nothing more than a pile of yellow bones and residual stretch marks. My ex-wife developed a disgusting-looking crown of stretch marks around her fatty midsection after giving birth to my beautiful girls, all of whom are with us today." He waved. "She hated the stretch marks more than Karma itself. Even after several plastic surgeries, they lingered like lobster claws engraved into her soft gut. God is good. Gentlemen, I assure you: life is not hopeless. There is always something ignoble to look forward to."

Other topics discussed at the Congress included nanomaterials, grapheme technologies, drug delivery systems and quantum dots.

Banal Story

Spitting out the seeds from an orange, L. Ron Hubbard caught his wife smiling in her sleep. He propped himself on an elbow, cocked his arm and punched her in the nose, believing she had been dreaming about another man. (NOTE: This essentially banal story can be applied to any situation and is in many kitchens a recipe for life. Roll it up and put it away in your pocket.)

Dear "King" David

Anthony:

I need to assassinate the emotional chromosomes that usurp the inequities of crazy GQ men. Yesterday I encountered another intermolecular stranger from the Clockwork World. She wanted to know about the location of panties in the store. Small in stature and dark in essence, she observed me with crushingly sincere eyes and laughed at my existential repartee. I took her hand and ushered her to the Consumer Gates. We joked about the panties—how they hung in the woods across the boulevard, how they reminisced undercrofts yet foreshadowed impossible afterlives. She said goodbye and I wept like a flogged macaque. Now the monkeys glint in the Xanax twilight. I can feel my underlip sinking into a jugular. Wish me luck.

Yours,
B.G.

Masturbation Video

Tracy Berringer just secured another restraining order against a previously unidentified stalker who sent her a masturbation video. Authorities have now identified the stalker as Los Angeles physiognomist and rapper **Dom Romero**.

[VIDEO]

According to a search warrant obtained by Hawgstrüffel Media, Romero, 44, had been dogging Berringer, 31, sending her threatening schizes. "I shoulda killed ®PoppyT that skeezy hoooooo," one of them read. He also schized: "I just bought a gun. Gonna get my license then get my pace, shoot that bitch in the face." In all cases, Romero argued that he had been testing out new lyrics in the schizoverse.

[VIDEO]

The search warrant makes it clear that Romero is deranged. He spends much of the 15-minute masturbation video discussing the head of his penis, the "character" of which he analyzes as if it were a human face. "Let's put a smile on that face," Romero intones on multiple occasions.

[VIDEO]

As we reported, Romero supplemented the video with a pic of himself standing in the driveway of Berringer's beach home in Malibu with a caption that read: "Outside yo house, bisnotch."

[PIC]

The warrant indicates that Berringer lives in fear. She is still on probation for her shoplifting conviction earlier this year and has only completed 30 minutes of the 400 hours of community service that she owes the state of California.

Authorities inform us that they hunted and captured Romero at a Motel 6 in Death Valley, Nevada, then ushered him back to L.A. and had him committed to a psychiatric hospital, where he remains.

Asteroid Rage

Decreased profits from space mining continue to harrow the private sector and have forced many companies to invest their time, effort and capital in deep space where the spoils are even more copious. Some asteroids boast payloads of nickel, iron and cobalt that total 100 trillion dollars. Companies such as Hawgstrüffel Media, funded by the likes of Cole Montgomery and John Travolta, have already launched satellites to search the universe for asteroids that promise the best harvests. Is this allowed? Is it legal? Can people own asteroids? Who has permission to mine them? Don't they need a license? The U.S. is in the process of devising unilateral and incomplete laws to "limit" the private ownership of asteroids. Fallout has been incendiary. Meanwhile China and Russia are drawing up their own laws. To what degree will their laws differ from U.S. laws? Whose laws will make more sense and ultimately be more effective? "The politics can't be known, but there will be politics," said Professor Glenn Freebird, a space-law specialist at the University of Michigan-Flint. The U.N. doesn't seem to care about the stance of investors and venture capitalists. Ideally spacefaring nations will work together to ensure that any citizen cannot "possess, own, transport, use and sell" asteroids, which is a human right by decree of the Space Launch Competitiveness Bill of 2015. Commercial activity remains in the capable hands of the International Telecommunications Union while trillions of dollars in minerals hang in the balance.

The Comfort of Shadows

Sergeant Bauer lunged forward, struck a pose, cradled the microphone like a newborn infant, and greeted the audience in an Elvis accent that lacked all traces of satire or burlesque. Hearty applause. He lost the accent and conducted the remainder of the seminar in his usual barreling, kindly brogue. "Say it like you mean it," he announced, and everyone repeated the words in a robotic drone: "I am not a man—I am dynamite." Hearty applause. Sergeant Bauer dove headlong into his routine, picking up where he had left off last week in Anaheim after providing context for newcomers. Recently a patient's Teacher told him from the Otherside that he could take on more clients. For years, every Teacher he contacted forbade it, avowing that it was not time to grow his practice and make money. He lived in near-poverty until he received news from "Kawika," the name of an especially sensitive patient's Teacher, that he could pursue materialistic gain. For good measure, he confirmed the information with "Halana" and "Wilikona" as their host bodies reclined like discarded ventriloquist dolls on lawn chairs in his basement office. Two months later he had exponentially multiplied his income and moved into an upper-floor suite in a Miami Radisson. Success felt as psychologically rewarding as it did morally and spiritually correct, but he didn't let it go to his head, knowing that the Details lurked behind the corners of every Turn. Usually he rehashed the advent of his spoils at least once per seminar. Today he became distracted by a spectator that produced gooseflesh on his forearms. The spectator did nothing to incite the reaction; a broad, plastic-looking jaw suggested that he may have a mild case of cherubism, but otherwise he sat in the second row, entirely non-threating, gazing at Sergeant Bauer with soft, attentive eyes. This happened several times a week. Gooseflesh almost always indicated positive energy and stemmed from a benevolent source, but not in this instance, and there was no question about the source. Somehow Sergeant Bauer found his way to the end of his discussion, yet he misspoke himself here and there, and he opted not to invite the congregation to join him in the abridged version of his introduction, which he invariably broadcasted in closing. "Man— dynamite," he whispered to himself and no one else, then paced into the comfort of shadows. Hearty applause.

Joel Osteen

Joel Osteen erupted in anger and stomped on a fan's head during a sermon. Now the victim wants justice.

Hawgstrüffel Media broke the story.

Anthony "King" David, 28, attended a service at the regional Gulf Campus of Lakeview Church in Galveston, Texas, on June 4. It's obvious that a fight broke out and something upset Reverend Osteen, who turned his shoe into a weapon.

[PIC]

It remains unclear if David initiated the fight. In light of recent events at Lakeview, Osteen doubtless rendered him collateral damage.

David told reporters that he checked into the hospital with pain in his neck and forehead. He plans to file a police report.

We reached out to Reverend Osteen's reps. So far, no word back.

Ghana Scammer (*In Medio Amore*)

About yourself is so interesting. You really look awesome. How I wish I am living closer to you for us to meet and talk in person rather than doing this online. I have so many words to say about what I like doing most. I am a very outgoing person who loves to dine out, travel, and enjoy the simple life. I am a hopeless romantic and very affectionate. I have a good sense of humor and I like to make you laugh. I love poetry, books, walks on the beach, and cozy candlelight dinners. I enjoy movies, television, music, traveling, the desert, the quietness of the mountains, the ocean, sunrises and sunsets. I like to chill out with a good book or watch a movie. Even more fun is to have a special someone to do this with. I am very easy to get along with and a very good listener. And honestly I am an honest heart that's looking for a stable relationship. I understand it is important to lay down lasting foundations for a long relationship. I am an active person who enjoys cycling and running best. I believe keeping fit is important. I am not interested in games or drama. Tell me more about yourself. Do you like to dance? I love to dance all styles: disco, house, or swing. I have attached some photos to this email. I hope you like how I look in those photos, and I hope to hear from you again.

[PICS]

Harmony and Discord

Neither Taiwanese nor Ukranian parliament entertained battle royals today, a surprise considering the traditionally hypertense nature of discussions about trade pacts with China. Typically pro- and anti-government lawmakers in both countries exchange punches and throw rubbish bins at one another for the sake of far less momentous issues and disagreements. The lack of violence has captured the attention of the First World. No matter what the subject in question may be, house speakers in both countries traditionally follow the same routine, rejecting the first bid to conduct a debate, which prompts one or more government officials to retaliate with highly aggressive verbal and then physical brutality. Their esteemed colleagues follow suit in an almost bored way, like abused animals who are expected to exert a certain allocation of pent-up aggression, although in general, these makeshift fight clubs see people beaten to unconscious pulps and, on occasion, killed. The procedure is well-known and parodied across the globe. Nothing of the sort happened in Taiwan or Ukraine on Wednesday, however, a freak act of synchronicity that nobody can explain. Such brazen peacefulness has instilled a deep anxiety in the collective consciousness regarding the direction of Taiwanese and Ukrainian parliament as well as the very apparatus of politics and government in economically viable countries. In some circles, the event has been labeled a crime against humanity and considered an attack on the dominant superpowers. Continued efforts to devolve into an Edenic zoo, sources say, may be punishable by law. The U.N. is currently investigating the matter as China persists in building its Arsenal of Superiority.

Au Pair

An au pair has been accused of decapitating a young girl under her care and then marching through the streets brandishing the head on a stick.

She said the killing was ordered by a mid-level sky-god named **Saul Flechsig**.

Hélène Kuragina, a French immigrant who resides in the Soviet republic of Falco, told a Moscow kommissar: "Flechsig will wreak the havoc of peace through my capable nerve-language."

Confined to a metal cage in the courtroom, she yawned and flirted with journalists.

The 45-year-old also complained that she was undernourished and would "die without breakfast."

Police arrested Kuragina, a mother of four, on Wednesday. She had been waving the child's severed head outside the Amadeus Metro Station by a pigtail.

Since her arrest, psychiatrists have been examining her.

Early reports indicate that Kuragina suffered from schizophrenia for over twenty years. Furthermore, she engaged in an incestuous relationship with her brother **Anatole Kuragin** at an early age.

The Einzelhaft Tribune claimed that she had recently become a disciple of Flechsig and spent most of her time chatting online with single men about the intermediate deity.

Kuragina's alleged victim, **Natasha Bolkonsky**, was four years old and suffered from cherubism and dyslexia.

Researchers claim that Kuragina murdered her in the guesthouse of her employer, Russian power couple **Andrei** and **Lisa Bolkonsky**, then set the guesthouse on fire and fled the scene.

According to bystanders, she said matter-of-factly, "Upon this rock I will build my church," and flung the head at a passing economy car.

Later Kuragina was seen begging for food and change on Drahdiwaberl Street.

She has been remanded in custody until her trial, the date of which is not yet determined.

Mindfulness

Brad Schmidt forgot how to smile and therefore forgot who he was. The owl-faced stranger that stared at him quizzically in the mirror—he didn't know this person, had never seen this person. He stared back and tried to make the stranger's mouth move, forcing the lip corners into the camber of nostrils ... He had attempted this before with inanimate objects. Much of his spare time was spent staring at inanimate objects and trying to telekinetically move them from point A to point B. He had never succeeded, but once he believed to have made a coffee mug twitch.

More problematic was the fact that everybody didn't try to make things move around with their minds. The first question he always asked women on dates, for instance, regarded their interest in and past experience with the practice of telekinesis. Not one woman had ever tried it, and they looked at him funny whenever he asked about it. How could everybody in the world—at least once in their lives, if not once a day—*not* try to move an object, inanimate or animate, using goddamned mind power? It baffled Brad Schmidt ... who, reflecting on his distaste for women who failed to dabble in telekinesis, and women in general, realized that his reflection—not the stranger, but the mentation—was a product of memory and therefore he had not technically forgotten himself. All was well.

Ungovernable Emotional Excess

Again—negatively charged gooseflesh.

Sergeant Bauer skips the accent, the mantra, the introduction. He ignores basal urges for pretense and performativity. He scours the audience for the interloper, the gatecrasher, the *persona non grata* ...

Purple suit. Green shirt. Green hair. White facepaint. Red lipstick. Frozen smile. Evil aura.

The Joker.

Unhinged, he asks him about the Joker outfit in an Elvis accent.

"What Joker outfit? Fuck're you talking about, asshole? Dipshit."

An angry Teacher leaps from Sergeant Bauer's bodysuit. Contrary to popular belief, it is not God. It calls itself "Ron."

Sergeant Bauer's body falls into a clump like a shrugged-off robe as "Ron" plunges into the audience and attacks the Joker.

A provisional exorcism follows a surprisingly gentle internment during which the Joker laughs at and taunts the motivational speaker's otherworldly protector and spectators cut for the exit doors. Several demons escape the Joker's Technicolor veneer; he disavows them, passing them off as remarkable "heavy metal" farts.

In the end, the Teacher smothers the Joker. His smile remains intact, of course, etched into the bleached bedrock of his face like a fossil.

When "Ron" returns to Sergeant Bauer, his body rises to a standing position as if lifted by a marionette string, then produces a bale of laughter from the chute of his mouth.

Finer Points of BRIAN GONKA's Sex Life Revealed in Indiana

BRIAN GONKA returned to a Dreamfield, Indiana, courtroom on Friday to be cross-examined by attorneys for Gapehole, a media website focusing on celebrity death. During his tenure on the stand, the wraith fielded questions about his sexual organs, rituals and desires.

Gapehole posted a three-and-a-half-minute clip of a sex tape in which BRIAN GONKA and **Gianna von Clamm**, daughter of lapsed antiquarian **B. Harrison von Clamm**, performed various sexual acts upon one another, some of which are currently illegal in the state of Indiana. The insurrections took place in a Muncie film studio, and BRIAN GONKA claims that he didn't know the cameras in the studio were turned on.

The Gapehole team spent four hours interrogating BRIAN GONKA, who answered questions put to him candidly in his renowned "Beyond the Veil" mezzo-soprano, which sounds like an insect with laryngitis speaking through a conch shell.

BRIAN GONKA approximated the number of women that he had slept with *ante* and *post mortem*. None of his answers corresponded with one another. Later, he told Hawgstrüffel Media that his failure to provide accurate information on every count had to do with an inability to recall how many women he had slept with as "an occupant of the desert of the real and the wasteland of the dead" and then tally up the numbers from both realms.

In addition to answering questions about the sex tape, the deceased man was required to read aloud passages from his autobiography, *Reign of the Grape Ape*. The prosecution insisted that certain passages authorized the production and release of the sex tape prior to its conception. Chief counsel **Dale Rabinowitz** also relayed clips from an explicit radio interview wherein BRIAN GONKA further incriminated himself by using "oversexualized rhetoric" in reference to von Clamm's "public parts."

BRIAN GONKA's longtime friend, Muncie filmmaker **Gordon Speck**, has been accused of orchestrating the scene and recording the footage behind everybody's back. He and Gianna von Clamm have been married for eighteen years. Prior to the sex tape going viral, she had been on the verge of finally changing her surname to "Speck" with the exception of retaining the preposition "von" as a "mnemonic placeholder."

Hours after Gapehole leaked the clip, BRIAN GONKA professed that he was in no way involved with the leak or the production of the sex tape. Moreover, he did not make the tape to profit from it.

Every major pornography corporation has assured BRIAN GONKA

that their checkbook is open and the sky is the limit, but BRIAN GONKA has yet to take the bait, quoting himself with pathological resolve: "The internet is **Zarathustra**. It lives forever. My dreams, my love, my hugs and my genitals—they will be sentenced to the prison of Zarathustra's jaws."

Executive Vice President for B.G. Planning **Herovit Bogg** stated: "In the wake of today's cross examination, it is clear that the undead soul of this former human male is a celebrity playing multiple roles. He is entitled to privacy in the private sector. Gapehole is suggesting that, if a celebrity plays a sexual role in a movie, it is acceptable and legal to film and publicize a sexual video of said celebrity in private. Celebrity has nothing to do with privacy and should not infringe upon one's right to it."

BRIAN GONKA died at the age of 67 from asphyxiation.

Fin du monde

Canadian actor **BRIAN GONKA** has been pronounced dead after being strangled in a stage hanging that went amiss.

The 67-year-old's family signed off on the donation of his organs, which doctors have removed, washed and prepared for transplantation, a spokesperson at Stratford General Hospital in Ontario told Hawgstrüffel Media subsidiary Zero Degrees Newsroom yesterday.

Police investigators are determined to ascertain whether or not safety procedures were followed, if they even existed in the first place.

A number of Canadian news agencies revealed that foul play may be involved. At least three suspects have been detained and are under investigation for manslaughter.

BRIAN GONKA had been performing in an experimental production of *Tetracycline* at the Avon Theater during the height of the Stratford Festival when an audience member realized that the rope around his neck might have been cutting off his breath. He wore a brown paper bag on his head when he leapt off of the box, but the spectator, **Janine Sokolowski**, 33, a female medical student at the University of Montreal, saw him quivering and deduced that something was wrong. She leapt onto the stage and untied the noose. Assisted by a stagehand, she lowered BRIAN GONKA to the floor.

Paramedics pronounced him dead upon arrival to the hospital, but the official word didn't come until later that evening. What remains of BRIAN GONKA will be cremated at the Third Ludavico Chapel on Monday. Theatergoers are hopeful that the actor will rise from his ashes and return to haunt the stage of life in the not-too-distant future.

ACT 4

ORDINARY DEMONS

Ghana Scammer (*Alius Tendo*)

My desires are simple. I like it if my man will be forever honest with me because I will be serving him like a maid. He will have to tell me some sweet words to turn me on, assuring me how special I am to him. He must look into my face and use his hand to play with my hair while kissing my lips and eventually kissing my chick. It will be fantastic. We can kill heaven by candlelight in the bedroom with some red flowers on the floor. You will play something cool and white while I dance in front of you naked and shaking my ass. Then my man will be telling me how sexy I am and how cute I look and how good my shape is. My man will praise me like a queen because there is no position in sex that I will not do for him to enjoy his lovemaking with me. Making love with the right man, the man that I will grow old with, is what I am searching for, so let's hope we meet in person one day soon.

Good Rehabilitation Facilities Make Good Neighbors

Accused of giving a cashier a dirty look as he paid for groceries, **Sebastian Angle** voluntarily checked himself into a rehabilitation facility, promising to do a better job of dealing with people and orienting his physiognomy. "Sometimes my face doesn't reflect what I'm actually thinking," he confessed to Hawgstrüffel Media correspondent Andrew Salvadore, "although that's no excuse. The further we evolve away from the Ape, the more the Ape seems to command us." Angle remained at the luxury facility in Tesla, New Mexico, for several hours, undergoing "intense therapy" that the chief psychologist said he took "as seriously as he did unconditionally." Upon release, however, Angle found himself inculpated in the lobby by an incoming patient who complained that he was breathing too hard and she couldn't hear herself think. "There are a lot of stairs in this place," he told Salvadore. "Like, a lot. And no elevators! How can there be no elevators in a 60-story building? I've been walking up and down stairways more than I have been getting therapy. Jesus." The director of the facility happened to be in the lobby at the time of Angle's utterance and lodged a complaint against him, worried about liability and "the rhetoric of empiricism"… Currently Angle exists in indefinite limbo. His latest film, a remake of the cult classic *Outlandos d'Amour*, premiers this Friday.

The Trigger

Can any man "trigger" attraction in a woman?

I used to debate this question with the other guys at work.

I saw girls chasing celebrities, rockstars and athletes because of their social status.

I saw girls getting turned on by rich guys, good-looking guys and "jacked" guys.

When I looked at myself in the mirror, I saw an OVERWEIGHT, BALDING, OUT-OF-SHAPE GUY with BAD SKIN and only enough SPARE CASH to last until the end of the month.

I said to myself: "Why would a woman want to open her legs for me?"

I started to wonder ...

Could a BELOW-AVERAGE GUY like me learn some lines, phrases, methods, stances, gestures and stories that would "trigger" attraction in any woman? Even without looks, money or muscles?

I am writing to tell you beyond the shadow of a doubt: the answer is YES ...

Honestly, some triggers worked and some fell flat.

Canned lines and routines—they bombed for me.

I'm sure there are guys who got them to work, but as I see it, they're tacky and turn women off.

I discovered that many other "triggers" actually worked in my favor.

This was the case in every situation with a girl, including starting a conversation, building chemistry and connection, getting her number, taking her on a date ... and of course working her over in the bedroom.

There are certain ways to act that always moved things forward and made her more attracted to me. And made her more comfortable with me. And made her want to get close to me.

AND MADE HER WANT TO SLEEP WITH ME.

And when I fully comprehended these triggers and brought them to the table, suddenly my SECOND-RATE LOOKS, my LOW INCOME, my BAD PHYSIQUE, my TERRIFIC BODY ODOR, my SMALL PENIS, my BALD HEAD, my SPOTTED GUMS and my SCHOOLBUS-YELLOW TEETH— none of it mattered anymore.

I WAS HOOKING UP WITH BEAUTIFUL GIRLS WHO USED TO BE OUT OF MY LEAGUE.

It never occurred to me to write a training manual for these techniques. I'm more of an "inner spatial" instructor. Then a friend of mine, Jack McGinnley, who had put these techniques to good use, took the initiative and wrote his own manual.

I think you'll learn a lot from it.

It tells you the best way to act to "trigger" attraction in a girl. It's great for 95% of guys who stare at the mirror and see somebody like me. We can't play the "looks and status" game, and we need to use words and body language wisely if we want to get girls into bed with us.

Jack calls it *Sexual Activation Blueprint* because it's a blueprint for how to activate female desire and get girls to sleep with you in a stealthy way. If used properly, you'll never receive another brutal rejection again.

This is high quality material. You can check it out here:

[VIDEO]

Best of luck,
BRIAN "The Trigger" GONKA

P.S. The video is totally hilarious. I can't be certain if the information regarding the U.S. government is actually true, although I have personally put *Sexual Activation Blueprint* to use and reaped its benefits. I would only recommend something that I believe will help you improve your life, and I'm happy to endorse it.

The Levee Was Dry

Dominus Bauer's wife stole a verse from "Amerikan Pie." Last Saturday night, she said to herself: *This will be the day that I die* ... Angelica Bauer has submitted paperwork for a restraining order from her partner of 20 years, explaining to authorities that he terrorized her for hours on September 3, massaging her temples and persuading her to commit treason. Angelica called 911 in hysterics; the operator says she breathed stertorously and shrieked for help. Shortly thereafter, the famous demigod was arrested for domestic violence. The victim claims that, during the assault, Dominus repeatedly uttered: "You don't fucking count." She also divulges that he massaged her temples too hard and now she has a permanent migraine. Dominus has been crude and violent before, insists Angelica. Signed legal documents indicate that he threatened her with a variety of firearms on multiple occasions in the past, barking, "I'll put you in a fucking rose garden you Vegas whore! I am one tough motherfucker and you can't bother me!" Angelica admits that he has been abusive in other ways, too, calling her "sugar tits" and making fun of her stretch marks, the sordid aftermath of birthing their six children.

Dominus returned to the limelight before this incident after his twenty-sixth reincarnation from smalltime obscurity in South Boston. By law, he must not interact with Angelica in any capacity; even visiting her many online profiles may result in prosecution.

Dominus Bauer

To: Dominus Bauer
From: BRIAN GONKA

Dominus:

I know you view the political sphere through the same lens as arctic divinities, but Bernie the Pharaoh has promised to install a postcapitalistic society. I'm scared, Dominus. I'm scared about the poisoned sandwich because I'm a man of my relentless word. I will go ex-pat if he's quietly assassinated by ordinary demons. My patience with this adolescent hellhole of a country is as thin as an insect's dick. The good news is that I am fast becoming close friends with my neighbor, a young medically retired marine who completed four tours in Azerbaijan and exhibits surprisingly mild symptoms of PTSD. Mind you, his psychodramatic wife is an Eskimo and shows no signs of transcending her roots. She lives in constant fear of hungry polar bears and overaggressive seals. This is compounded by her devout animist faith and the potential dangers involved in killing a polar bear or a seal even if one is trying to eat you because some of these precarious animals might possess souls not unlike human beings. Her thesis: there is no greater crime than releasing a soul from a body against the soul's will. Translation: the soul is the prison of the body, etc., etc. Despite her general paranoia and indisposition, though, she never judges me, and I feel like her husband and I could hobble mountains. He is a sincere maniac.

Apologies in advance for the fatalist enthusiasm of a blue-collar enzyme.

Ghana Scammer
(*Finis*)

[PIC]

[ACCOUNT NUMBER + ROUTING]

Ghana Scammer (*Epilogus*)

I was too stupid to fall for a lady from Ghana about six months ago and I did send her thousands of dollars. All the romancers from that country are scammers—much worse than Nigerians. Last week I found out that it's run by organized crime bosses from Russia. They have a studio where those ladies train how to talk to men and ask for money. Most of the time, men control their laptops and they type for them. I sent $100 to a lady and I got all the information and a few videos of me chatting with those ladies. They record all of it and they threaten to post naked pictures of you on the internet if you don't send them money. When you chat with them, please pay attention and make sure there is a laptop on the screen. How is that possible? They have a man in the background with a video camera. This studio is really used to make porno movies and the set includes a bedroom, bathroom, kitchen and all the other rooms they need to make you believe that you are chatting with a real person in a real house where people can have sex. Guys—please do not fall for their story and do not send any money. You can lose everything. I tried to send more money yesterday and Western Union blocked me and closed my bank account.

Nietzsche's Crusade

Plagiarizing the favorite stunt of drummer **Keith Moon**, who died in 1978 at the age of 32 from a clomethiazole overdose, everyman **BRIAN GONKA**, age variable, has taken to flushing powerful explosives down toilets in order to "measure the scatological import of the ensuing pyrotechnics." Hawgstrüffel Media broke the story. BRIAN GONKA began what he referred to as "Nietzsche's Crusade" with cherry bombs but quickly graduated to M-80 fireworks and sticks of dynamite. The destruction hypnotizes him, sources say. As hunks of porcelain and offal fly through the air, BRIAN GONKA howls and cackles like the Joker, and sometimes he masturbates into the wreckage. Efforts to arrest BRIAN GONKA or even curb his behavior have been in vain; somehow he evades authorities despite the prevalence of his celebrity. For the time being, no toilet in any hotel or changing room is safe.

Death of the Space Age, Dawn of the Grape Ape

The igneous dreams of yesterday have ceased to become the electronic realities of tomorrow. Only the shape of heaven remains.

Three. Two. One.

GONKAPOCALYPSE

This is an effort to forego the skin and foreground the skull. The GONKAFICATION of the universe extends beyond the outer limits (i.e., the "Veil"). **Dominus Bauer** is powerless against it despite being a man who became himself. There are no viable domini in this New Eden. **BRIAN GONKA** originated as a Bad Idea gestating in the Wrong Thinktank. Postpartum depression lasted eight years; then the subject devolved into human form like a fallen apple rotting on a bed of crabgrass in a timelapse video. Everybody in the room makes a concerted effort to identify with their own persona, experimenting with an array of socially acceptable facemasks. The result: lackluster Jekyll v. Hyde. Brutal and anxious, BRIAN GONKA panhandles for cash at a Quality Dairy. He is worth millions but enjoys the Game, brooding on certain images until they become monstrously unrecognizable and allow him to inhabit the psychoses of several outpatients in one breath. Later, reading a stolen newspaper, BRIAN GONKA guffaws and blows wine through his nose onto the Want Ads. He blew his nose with the same force of presence last May. I remember. Running from the sky, he burst vessels in both eyes. He looked more like the twenty-second BRIAN GONKA than the forty-eighth BRIAN GONKA of which there are infinitudes.

[PIC]

I am BRIAN GONKA. You are BRIAN GONKA. Like **Colonel Kurtz**. Like **Captain Ahab**. And yet there is only one BRIAN GONKA, just as there is one Dominus Bauer, one alchemical afterlife, etc.

[PIC]

BRIAN GONKA's bad breath supersedes his body odor. BRIAN GONKA is a licensed autoscopist who encounters different versions of himself in every room of the brothels he commandeers and remakes in his own image. BRIAN GONKA hurls furniture at people without motive, inciting petty wrongdoers to belie the cult of Shanghai dreams. I refuse to acknowledge the egregious teeth of the wall mice in BRIANK GONKA's 100-year-old house. The vermin are as lifeless, ghostly, Lovecraftian and antagonistic as the homeowner himself. "The Future Is History's Lapdog," reads the sign over the front door. For at least three centuries, the soul of BRIAN GONKA leaped from one ventriloquist doll to another, banned from the country club of human flesh. Once he materialized in an ATD (Anthropomorphic Test Device) en route to the Eighth Wall at 120 mph. He experienced the pain of impact in every electric sensor and polyvinyl fiber of his being. **L. Ron Hubbard** was BRIAN GONKA's symbolic father and effective **Darth Vader**, only instead of cutting off his hand, he castrated him so that the boy couldn't enact Oedipal revenge. He had five siblings and "Hubbard" beat and cursed the children like **Richard Nixon** on the White House tapes. He paid special attention to BRIAN GONKA, who he hated the most and, for unknown reasons, only communicated with and castigated in a bastardized Italian lingo reminiscent of certain spaghetti westerns. In effect, BRIAN GONKA believes that there's something about the Italian language that produces mafia-like behavior. All behavior is linguistically oriented, according to BRIAN GONKA, and the descant of Italian morphemes and phonemes in particular conjures the desire for an excess of violence, territorialism, misogyny, hairdos and family. My supervisor agrees. He has slipped into that radical zone watching a story on "60 Minutes" about printing 3D cellular tissue from a portable stereolithograph in order to replace rotten, devolved, or otherwise malignant ensembles of like-minded cells. Histopathology reports expose nothing but the psychological truth, a product of the imagination. Memories are like holidays: nothing good comes from their procedural deployment. As a child, BRIAN GONKA played the role of Bully as much as Target, hammering meek-looking turds with one hand while fending off big black sonsofbitches with the other. Periodically he would defend himself from himself. Before the gums spit down the fangs, he remembered observing numerous "defective peers" with a kind of innocent distaste and belligerence. The way an underlip jutted out or a swath of acne scarred a cheek invoked primordial enmity in him. He wanted to batter the owner of those imperfections. *Nihil.* The desire didn't belong to him. It belonged to his cells. To his archeopsychic past.

[VIDEO]

BRIAN GONKA can run faster than an Ovidian god while drinking a beer. When you chase him, he always gets away, thirst slaked. In fact, he runs much slower with empty hands, contemplating the plight of **Anthony "King" David**, his favorite Hebrew, and the masculine angst that he so freely sublimates and turns into gospel. BRIAN GONKA is weary of judgment and the girls who deliver him expressions that oscillate between technocratic fuck-me-please smiles and quasi-terrified stay-the-fuck-away-from-me glances, as if he might be a dog on a leash. Society, he regularly opines, functions on the turn-table of a Cartesian, binary, schizoid split—**Jean-Paul Sartre** called it *La faille merdique* ("The Shitty Rift")—brought to bear by the alienation of subject and object. If only a woman's curves were enough. BRIAN GONKA tries with great difficulty to distract himself. The recent death of his cat, **Erwin the Cat**, spurred an accumulation of sorrow that appears to have no endpoint in sight. And yet death matters only insofar as the media punctuates and publicizes its banal repartee. Whenever a possible suitor makes wisecracks about BRIAN GONKA, he prays for her to contract breast cancer, and notwithstanding Dominus Bauer's supernatural interventions, his prayers usually come true. Dominus Bauer relies on Teachers to set the record straight. They speak in fluid tongues through scores of flesh puppets. He milks the rhetoric like darkness from an udder. Over and over the Teachers announce that God wants him to rot in Midwestern Indiana or Ohio until he is an old man at which point he may perform chiropractic, motivational speaking and exorcism anywhere in the universe.

[VIDEO]

As the conclusion of the footage suggests, Kratom (*mitragyna speciosa*), a Southeast Asian leaf that stimulates the brain's opioid receptors and functions like heroin, can induce vivid dream states in which halfass goblins chase the protagonist through the hallways of vast crumbling sanatoriums. Sometimes there are secret societies of shapeshifters, one of whom the protagonist falls in love with and unintentionally marries in a semi-comatose trance at a casino chapel in Vegas. The Elvis who presides over the ceremony is drunk on Mai Tais. Afterwards he repeatedly attempts to cajole BRIAN GONKA into reading his screenplay, mistaking the Slender Man for a successful filmmaker. BRIAN GONKA politely deflects the solicitations while inspecting his cellphone and trying to remain conscious.

[DICK PIC]

[DICK PIC]

[DICK PIC]

Dominus: I realize now that BRIANK GONKA is the name of Digitized Death, my Secret Saint of Mediated Dread. I am grateful that you are dismembering my memory of him. He breaks into my apartment several times a week when I am asleep and leaves me notes, signing and dating them, as if to etch them into the copperplate of eternity. For example:

"I would kill myself if I had your mustache."
—BRIAN GONKA, 1:28 a.m., Monday, July 17

"My breakfast is more interesting than your dreams."
—BRIAN GONKA, 3:15 a.m., Friday, September 8

"Why are you stealing my experimental recipes for wine?
Why are you stealing my power?"
—BRIAN GONKA, 2:44 a.m., Thursday, October 12

"I want to see that final look in a dead man's eyes.
That's why I love you."
—BRIAN GONKA, 5:01 a.m., Sunday, December 24

The last assertion irked me like a mosquito holocaust. The man nearly took my life, after all. I read his diary. I read his poems. I read his bathroom-stall graffiti. Everything had to do with a borderline erotic fixation on my future corpse. Concerns regarding my skull, dead or alive, are another matter. This has been the nightly Purge Report, starring BRIAN GONKA, who plays all of the roles yet altogether evades the Performance. Truth is as much his weapon as his engine. The man is not a man. He is a sick reptile who dimly remembers the cheap suit of his human incarnation.

GONKA SEE GONKA DO

Test subject 7531 BRIAN GONKA is responding well to the retro-dipsomanic stimuli. This morning he failed to consume one 12 oz. can of Miller Genuine Draft in a practicable span of microseconds. Vengeful scientists immediately delivered 400 joules of taser reinforcement to his testicular pouch, mitigating an instantaneous telepathic ingestion of the Champagne of Beers. The results are curious. Since lunchtime, 7531's gaze has consumed seventy-two 12 oz. cans of MGD, plus four 22 oz. bottles of Colt 45 and a pint of Wild Turkey. The preemptive simian Eden of his corneas has now degraded into a lazy, amphibious malevolence. He remains cold-blooded—but not thick-skinned, contrary to the board of trustees' original profile of the subject.

ROMEO GONKA

Dominus Bauer met his fellow implantees at a schizo-anonymous meeting in the basement of a pre-depression era cottage owned by a former Baptist preacher who survived a backstreet lobotomy. BRIAN GONKA attended the procedure, idly shapeshifting from animal to man to insect as he hovered above the furnace like an inflected Buddha. Deferred auditory phantoms had been buried in the air. Dominus Bauer nodded off and on until he heard the confession of a whore in the wind: "Hallucination seemed more logical than ratiocination. Then I noticed an incongruity in my pineal gland. Postdimensional life forms were forcibly inverted into my optic nerve. They called themselves 'Romeo Gonka,' but I knew they were BRIAN GONKA, and they confiscated the laboratory of my psyche. Since then, I can't stop fingering myself. Here is the denominator of the fraction, as it were. The numerator—mankind ..."

GONKADEMIC (CODA)

Last night I violated curfew. I needed a beer. During a half-hour nap, BRIAN GONKA drank three cases of MGD, grew weary, entered my abdomen and sampled my plasma. I staggered into the bonfire-constellated streets in a hypnogogic stupor as the orphans of the simulacrum spun uptown in furious roundelays. They sang and danced and ignored me ... and I felt a recombination. It was accompanied by a small token of gratitude, the benefactor of which showed me his secret name.

[INTERMISSION]

Reduced to gristle, Dominus Bauer leaks evil from the Veil of his erstwhile prowess. Nothing changes but the tides and the seasons.

TRACTOR JAW

In light of recent events, BRIAN GONKA's renowned "attaché" and self-proclaimed "scavenger of half-dead dreams" confirmed rumors of the plague as an active experience, the moving image as an immortal wraith who is worth his price in sweat. TRACTOR JAW was discovered gutting, scaling and fileting perch on a sidewalk near Lock One Theater in an effort to entertain consumers. As always, his rhetoric fell short of outstripping his wits. For example:

"I felt the presence of harpies. They yanked me from my trailer and showed me the speaking ruins."
—TRACTOR JAW, 10:51 p.m., Saturday, August 26

"I'm tired of perspiration. My triumvirate is hungry and undying."
—TRACTOR JAW, 11:46 p.m., Saturday, August 26

"If my hands are tied behind my back, my teeth will become a talisman of unspeakable power."
—TRACTOR JAW, 11:57 p.m., Saturday, August 26

"Ben Affleck is a good fucking Batman. Seriously."
—TRACTOR JAW, 12:01 a.m., Sunday, August 27

Many overexposed consumers have suffered from various fits of synesthesia; above all, they claim not be able to get the scent of TRACTOR JAW out of their ears. The symptoms do not appear to be debilitating or contagious, however, and all infected parties are expected to return to normal within the year.

Thus Fowl Precedes Fermentation

Dominus Bauer is rebooted as an IRS law enforcement investigator. Dominus Bauer is rebooted as an Assistant Professor of Art History. Dominus Bauer is rebooted as a reality show cook. First task: acquire cutlery. Second task: sharpen cutlery. Third task: learn how to throw cutlery. Fourth task: throw cutlery at all adversaries, opponents, antagonists, assailants, aggressors, provocateurs, raconteurs, admen, baristas, lighting technicians, grifters ... Sixth task: repeat sequence *ad infinitum*. Seventh task: Brainstorm new recipes ... Pairings and plates materialize and deliquesce on the screen of his imagination. He settles on an unlikely twosome: wine and eggs. He mediates the offbeat collision of tastes by introducing a new strain of Red Bali Kratom. He tests the strain backstage, ingesting 25 grams dissolved in hot water with grapefruit juice, a Kratom potentiator. Dressed like a sixteenth century warlock, he saunters into the onstage kitchen and greets applause with a humble bow. He pours himself a glass of red zinfandel and cracks several eggs into a pan. It isn't a nonstick pan. The producers had guaranteed him a nonstick pan. Enraged, Dominus Bauer hurls knives at the audience, one after another, tapping a seemingly inexhaustible supply and screaming in an extinct tongue. CAMERA ZOOMS IN to EXTREME CLOSE-UPS when the knives find purchase and blood spurts from bullseyes in SLOW MOTION ... Series of FLASHBULB INTERCUTS and FREEZEFRAMES involving superstylized butchery ... At the climax of the episode, Dominus Bauer is rebooted as a nomadic sommelier, but all he can think about as he hitchhikes from town to town is whether or not to scramble the eggs, turn them into an omelet, or make them over easy, cooking them just long enough so that forking the yokes barely makes them drool onto the flaccid ivory beaches of their physiques. Thus fowl precedes fermentation.

Law and Order

These are their stories.

    Fade in.

    Fucking in an alley, two people discover a dead body.

EXT.STREET – DAY

    DETECTIVE GONKA: Looks like my last date. Flat on her back with a knife in her cunt. And I'm only on my second cup of coffee.

    Detective Bauer sweeps Detective Gonka off his feet with a knee wheel. They wrestle around the crime scene, staining the evidence with their identities. Officers who try to break up the fight succumb to a deterministic chaos wherein their bodies are assimilated into the "plot" of one of Detective Gonka's many internal narratives. Slowly the fight evolves from a spectacle of physical to rhetorical aggression. Chainsmoking cigarettes, Detective Bauer and Detective Gonka attempt to out-nuance and out-modulate one another as they utter prerecorded lines like units of density from an effete dimension. Nobody wins, and Detective Gonka reshuffles the poker deck of his subjectivity.

    DETECTIVE GONKA: Hit me.

    Dies.

Executive Producer
DARYL FOLKENFLICK

Message from God

I don't need money. I only need $ex. I understand perfect dirty mechanics. I am a good woman. I am discreet when dating in your area. I am available to swap nude selfies and hook up with you for FREE. I wish to flirt with you—we will never forget this adventure. Darling: there are many lessons I must teach you. My dearest: we will not tell anybody if you have an affair. I am not your neighbor. I am wild. I am private. I am a MILF. I think our $ex could be a great experience under the sky. I want to hang out with you. I look forward to moaning with pleasure. Please email me directly. I would like to engage in an anal encounter. I have urgent information for you. It will benefit your entire family. I cannot wait to show you my busty tits. Hurry. How glad I will be hearing from you. I am interested in getting to know you and that is a good idea. I am delighted by our future. I admire your gentle way. May I be your friend?

Sisyphus II: The Sequel

Minutes after being incarcerated, I got shanked.

Seconds later, another inmate shanked me.

Security guards ushered me to the medical ward and shanked me before they left.

The doctor entered the operation chamber and shanked me, operated on me, and shanked me.

I went to see the warden and he was hiding behind his office door and he jumped out and screamed and shanked me.

Back to the medical ward.

A volley of nurses shanked me, taking methodical turns. They emptied my body into a garbage chute and I slid down a long metal spillway into a dumpster where several sleeping homeless men awoke and shanked me. They threw me out of the dumpster and I landed on a cop car. Two plainclothes officers got out and circled the vehicle like sharks. They arrested me and dragged me into a court room to stand in front of the same judge who had incarcerated me that morning. He slammed the gavel against the sound block before I even stated my purpose, then ordered the bailiff to shank me and put me in the hole.

I escaped.

The alarm went off and everybody threw makeshift knives at me as I ran away and took refuge in my parents' basement.

One night I woke up and they were looking at me, deciding what to do.

Mother shanked me first, and I died.

At the funeral, the minister said a few words and everybody bent over and shanked me as they lowered my body into the grave.

Beyond the Veil, a demon convinced me that he was my Teacher, lured me close and shanked me. I experienced a long period of depression and anxiety prior to rebirth.

Outside the womb, the doctor gripped me by the ankles, spanked me, and shanked me ...

Question and Addition

Do your sources indicate any hard data of abuse beyond our chronic absence? I forgot to express my concerns about the doomed monkey, which is fitting—the monkeygeist, so to speak, fleetingly glimpsed ...

Marginalization

And my dead brother used to overwhelm me in my early teens. The Scorpion Contortion suited him best. He was captain of the high school wrestling team. He used to hold me down and drape his long coccyx across my nose. One day, triumphantly, I discovered that I had grown old enough to break his face with a head butt. All this reminded me of that polemical comedy. It nearly crucified me. At the same time, my pathological unconscious flitted across the television screen like outtakes from a bad noir movie. Lyrical exorcisms allowed me to thwart the absent father-monster unto/into death. I'm surprised I escaped with all my limbs and ideas intact. FYI.

APBs

Dominus ———— is rebooted as an underwear model despite a large, disproportionate potbelly. Tourists who wander by the studio grip the potbelly and shake it, producing an uncanny sensation in both Dominus ———— and the user. He tells the tourists that he is "empty and happy." In contrast, neither hide nor hair has been seen of his doppelgänger, his Teacher, or his psychological father. This is the way of all media, although the last sighting of every character in question took place within the same hour on the second Wednesday of a fortnight traffic jam in Indonesia. More popular rumors locate each character in the ethereal captivity of a semi-sentient, possibly evil wind that kicked up and incorporated their essence for sale on the black market. Authorities have put out an APB in hopes of renegotiating terms. Worst case scenario: the business of life will not stand face-to-face with its opposable objects (i.e., dreams and death). At best, God will bear another son on earth, but this messiah will fly underneath the radar, refusing to impart wisdom about his origins or existence even to urchins and charity cases living under the street. Effectively, another APB will have to be put out on God. Victoria's Secret must be unlocked and exposed on deep space satellite channels. And yet evolution has taught us not to see the real world for what it really is; our sensoria have been trained to lie to us, lest our molecules experience the horror of subdermal geometry. This is the universe from core to outer limit. So must we usher truth into the abattoir of extinction (i.e., distinction).

I Died Last Week

The signature of the cult icon's death reverberated for centuries. It could not be adequately staged or summarized, however, and eventually it became an active record.

He admitted that he had been "preparing to die for several millennia" after being diagnosed with a rare form of consciousness, according to reports in Celina, Ohio, his place of residence.

"He was often in a state of nominal awareness," said **Bill Steinberg,** a neighbor who brought him groceries when he felt too wakeful to leave the safety of his 600-acre estate. "I could tell that his body temperature had neither dropped nor escalated. He seemed very weak and disoriented as a result."

Hawgstrüffel Media followed up with the star of *The Upholstered Apocalypse*'s family.

"He regularly processed thoughts, and when he didn't, we assumed he was daydreaming," said his estranged half-brother, **Archibald Wink**, 35.

"The angle of his discontent had nothing to do with his fine-tuned subjectivity or the conventional ways in which he perceived the world and its inhabitants," said his estranged sister, **Maizy Smith**, 40.

Confined to a wheelchair by Lou Gehrig's disease, his mother, **Embeth Bruns**, 72, said, "He never cried. Ever. He only stared and breathed."

Primary, secondary and third-party family members are currently at war over a $250 million fortune.

Due to his faith in cognizance, the deceased personality refused medical treatment, believing he could be cured by "transgressive behavior," by which he meant "acting on his own recognizance."

Pink skin hung from the tips of the 44-year-old's heavy fingers as he was cremated last Friday in a private ceremony attended by only one family member, Celina florist **Nelson Tyco**, 48.

Tributes have been pouring in.

He is being remembered all over the world.

The rights to the belvedere of his psyche remain up for grabs. An auction will be held on Thursday at Brew Nation Potter House on Main where he spent ample time drinking Kratom tea and craft beer while gazing absently out the window at the municipal courthouse across the street. The self-proclaimed "thinker" was notoriously fond of architecture.

F451

21-year-old elementary schoolteacher **Brenda Diamond** died last night at 2:54 a.m. from burn injuries sustained on June 7 when she was set on fire for refusing a marriage proposal, police reported.

Ordered to commit the crime by Diamond's rebuffed suitor, television personality **Gil Stoppard**, eight Portuguese hitmen beat her with two-by-fours, then poured gasoline over her body and set it ablaze, the victim's family told Hawgstrüffel Media.

"Brenda was at home babysitting her 6-year-old brother while her parents attended a funeral in Dreamfield," said her aunt, **Marisa Stillwater**. "I got a text message telling me that she was 'on fire.' I thought it was an accident, like a gas pipe broke or something."

Accompanied by anxious grievers, her parents left the funeral, sped home to the Indianapolis suburb of Alphaville in central Indiana, and discovered Brenda lying on the kitchen floor. Burns covered 90% of her body, according to forensic experts.

The hitmen loitered at the scene and were immediately taken into custody, said police inspector **Dennis Diamond**, who is unrelated to the victim. Blood tests revealed that they had ingested large quantities of Green Malay Kratom in the vicinity of 40 grams apiece.

"The roads in Alphaville were closed for construction and we had to carry Brenda on a rubber mat to the nearest highway where an ambulance picked her up," said **Cornelius Stillwater**, an uncle. "Her skin and flesh was falling off and we had to be careful. By the time we got to the highway, she didn't even look human."

Doctor's stabilized the young woman upon arrival at Parkview Regional Medical Center, but the extent of her injuries was beyond repair. "She expired in due course," proclaimed the chief of surgery, **Dr Nathan Benway**.

Police inspector Diamond reminded the public that the arrest warrant for Stoppard, who evaded capture, remains in effect. He urged the killer to turn himself in, anxious that people may resort to vigilantism in order to avenge Brenda's horrific murder.

"Violence against women has tripled in the last six months," said **J.J. Marvel-Ann**, a spokesperson for the Independent Human Rights Commission of Indianapolis.

In March, **Leonardo DiCaprio** accidentally set fire to his girlfriend, Swiss supermodel **Zoe Gamma**, during a public squabble. The incident gained worldwide recognition as DiCaprio went on a two-month apology tour throughout Europe and the Caribbean, warning fans about the dangers of playing with fire.

Since the conclusion of the tour in Navagio Beach, Greece, police have formally investigated upwards of 100 cases of women being set on fire in Indiana alone, according to the commission's latest report.

Attack Therapy

In an attempt to sanitize the mind-body apparatus and cleanse it of any residual demons, literal or metaphorical, producing what Scientologists might refer to as a "Clear," BRIAN GONKA exposes the psychological vulnerabilities of the Hive, assuring the planet that self-destruction is as much a matter of rage as hope. The fundamental desire for affirmation and growth marks every step we take towards the Abyss. BRIAN GONKA is the symptom. The disease and the cure are superfluities.

Man Accused of Spraying Grocery Store Food with Mouse Poison

Beyond memory, there is only ideology and desire. None of it has any bearing on reality or history ...

The Kratom retailer misappropriated my authority.

I ordered 120 grams of Borneo on Wednesday morning and paid for express delivery.

It won't arrive until Monday.

This is fine. I am always prepared for the worst.

Since infancy, I have been full of spleen.

My neighbor's PTSD concerns me. I feel something for the man. He's a liar and tries to kill me at least once a week.

Perhaps I should introduce him to K., which will exorcize his pain ...

In the baking aisle, I entertain another messiah complex. My bust materializes on all of the cereal boxes and milk cartons in the grocery store.

Ruined, customers bleed from the nostrils, ears and eyes as they move beyond the Veil.

Le ténébreux.

The bruises and scratches on my face look like the aftermath of a duel with a raccoon. I blame my condition on a champagne bottle attack at a liquor store.

They don't believe that story.

They insist that I injured myself in a drunken rage, fornicating with the gods of yesteryear.

As always—tomorrow is another day. The future may be uncertain, but nobody can discount the certitude of oblivion ...

I return to the house of my parents, who have invited mankind to live in the basement.

Everybody is talking about my organs, my blood cells, my molecules and my atoms.

Everybody wants to be me on the inside.

When I escape my body, I encounter my flesh.

This is the moment of supreme tension.

This is when I find myself, forget myself ...

Who is that garden-variety *übermensch*?

Surely his net worth reflects his great and hollow interior.

Poisoned with age, he gazes out the window of the keep on the gray lake.

A sparkling bar of sunlight divides the lake into two unequal halves like the vinculum of a perverse fraction. Across the lake, children lie on the beach and make angels in the sand as bored demons make noise in the surf, haunting the water and signaling the earth.

Three. Two. One.

Xerox.

An anxious comparison with the possible results will only reveal what is already unborn.

"A sharp report from the madhouse is always a joy. Wilson's prose is exquisitely precise and his humor relentlessly unpredictable. Only two other authors have made me laugh out loud so often: William S. Burroughs and Spike Milligan. *Natural Complexions* is a very funny, very smart book."

—**MALCOLM MC NEILL**, author of *Tetra, Observed While Falling* and *Reflux+*

"In these exquisite flares of literary highwire, D. Harlan Wilson corkscrews facts into helixes of strange that feel realer than truth."

—**MATTHEW ROBERSON**, author of *List, Impotent* and *1998.6*

"D. Harlan Wilson's vignettes sometimes read like news reports from a Fortean America, sometimes read like the dream journals of daytime television personalities, but are always disconcertingly and hilariously connected to the present… reality. Wilson explains how a mysterious tornado can get a shoplifter cleared of charges, an ill-advised selfie can set your world on fire, and discovering the sixth person pronoun can revive a celebrity's career. In each case the stories he tells are both absurd and true."

—**DOUGLAS LAIN**, author of *After the Saucers Landed, Last Week's Apocalypse* and *Bash Bash Revolution*

"An author in the revolutionary tradition, which he's unafraid to satirise as venomously as every other."

—**LOUIS ARMAND**, author of *The Combinations*

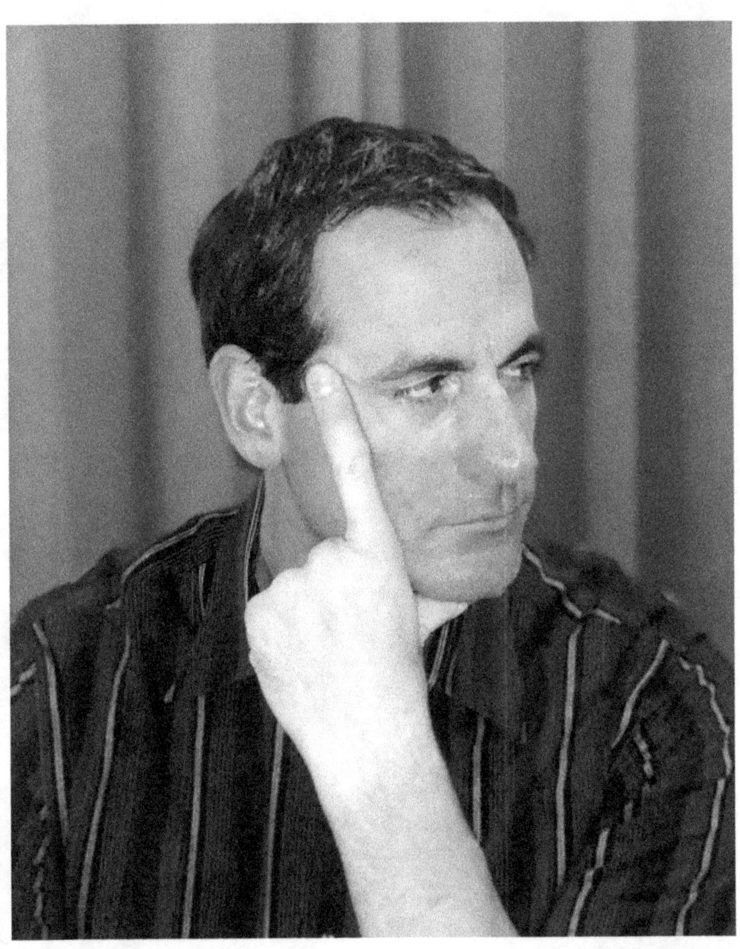

D. HARLAN WILSON is an American novelist, short-story writer, literary critic, playwright, editor & university professor. He is the author of over twenty book-length works of fiction & nonfiction, & more than a thousand of his stories, essays & reviews have appeared in magazines, journals & anthologies across the world in multiple languages.

www.dharlanwilson.com

www.equuspress.com

www.ingramcontent.com/pod-product-compliance
Lightning Source LLC
Chambersburg PA
CBHW070317120726
47910CB00007B/2517